FIFE LIBRARIES CENTR
KU-529-371

SPECIAL MESSAGE TO READERS

This book is published under the auspices of

THE ULVERSCROFT FOUNDATION

(registered charity No. 264873 UK)

Established in 1972 to provide funds for research, diagnosis and treatment of eye diseases. Examples of contributions made are: —

A new Children's Assessment Unit at Moorfield's Hospital, London.

•

Twin operating theatres at the Western Ophthalmic Hospital, London.

•

A Chair of Ophthalmology at the University of Leicester.

•

The establishment of a Royal Australian College of Ophthalmologists "Fellowship".

You can help further the work of the Foundation by making a donation or leaving a legacy. Every contribution, no matter how small, is received with gratitude. Please write for details to:

THE ULVERSCROFT FOUNDATION,
The Green, Bradgate Road, Anstey,
Leicester LE7 7FU, England.
Telephone: (0116) 236 4325

In Australia write to:
THE ULVERSCROFT FOUNDATION,
c/o The Royal Australian College of Ophthalmologists,
27, Commonwealth Street, Sydney, N.S.W. 2010.

CORDOBA'S TREASURE

The man was near to death when he appeared at the Fullers' homestead. He carried with him part of the legendary Cordoba's Treasure, but before he could say where he got it, he died. Wes Hardiman and Ben Travis, sent to investigate, got more than they bargained for when they rode into Dry Ridge, a town living in fear. The two men learn the secret of Cordoba's Treasure, but not before bullets fly and they put their own lives at risk.

ALAN C. PORTER

FIFE LIBRARIES CENTRAL AREA WITHDRAWN

CORDOBA'S TREASURE

Complete and Unabridged

LINFORD
Leicester

First published in Great Britain in 1995 by
Robert Hale Limited
London

First Linford Edition
published 1996
by arrangement with
Robert Hale Limited
London

The right of Alan C. Porter to be identified as
the author of this work has been asserted by him
in accordance with the
Copyright, Designs and Patents Act, 1988

Copyright © 1995 by Alan C. Porter
All rights reserved

British Library CIP Data

Porter, Alan C.
Cordoba's treasure.—Large print ed.—
Linford western library
1. English fiction—20th century
2. Large type books
I. Title
823.9′14 [F]

ISBN 0-7089-7951-3

Published by
F. A. Thorpe (Publishing) Ltd.
Anstey, Leicestershire

Set by Words & Graphics Ltd.
Anstey, Leicestershire
Printed and bound in Great Britain by
T. J. Press (Padstow) Ltd., Padstow, Cornwall

This book is printed on acid-free paper

To Katherine Emily; a new niece and a new sister for Paul and Heather

KIRKCALDY DISTRICT LIBRARIES
319118
FIFE LIBRARIES CENTRAL AREA WITHDRAWN

1

HE came at sundown!

Just as Meg and Jesse Fuller were preparing to eat their evening meal, the door of their lonely homestead flew open and he stood braced in the doorway. A wild-looking, half-naked individual clad only in a pair of ragged pants. The sun had burnt and blistered the thin, wasted body, scorching the flesh into white, leaking blisters. Behind a dark tangle of lank, matted hair that partially obscured his face, dark eyes peered with feverish intensity.

Meg screamed and came to her feet, chair tipping over with a clatter behind her. She pushed whitened knuckles against her lips. Jesse was on his feet as the ragged figure, breathing harshly, lurched into the room on feet that were cut and bleeding, rubbed raw to the bone in places. He clutched a small linen-wrapped bundle in one thin, dirty hand that he refused to release even when, after two faltering steps, he collapsed face down on the wooden floor.

Jesse, a big, rawboned farmer, considered going for his scatter-gun, on hooks over the fireplace, but changed his mind as the man fell. He darted around the table and Meg gasped as she joined him, grabbing his arm with a trembling hand. The man's back was a lattice of hideous weals that criss-crossed the flesh and could only have been made by a whip. Jesse patted her hand and knelt by the man, gently turning him over.

"Get water, woman," he called. Meg fled to the table, filled a glass from a jug and handed it to Jesse. Supporting the man, Jesse dribbled water on to dry, cracked lips that were scabbed and oozing blood.

The stranger's eyes flickered open

and his Adam's apple danced as he swallowed gratefully.

"What happened to you, mister? Who are you?" Jesse asked.

The scabby lips parted.

"Mal . . . Mal . . . Mallinson." The weak, barely audible voice was thick and slurred.

"Gotta get you to a doctor, mister," Jesse said soothingly, at the same time wondering how. The nearest doctor was in Dry Ridge and that was twelve miles to the south-west.

Mallinson raised the small, flat bundle and pushed it towards Jesse who handed the glass to Meg in order to take the object.

"Cordoba's Treasure." Mallinson drew in a shuddering breath. A greyish pallor had spread across the sun-ravaged flesh, leaching the colour from it; Jesse knew that Mallinson was not far from death. "Give . . . give it to, — " The whispering voice tailed away. The ravaged body gave a convulsive shudder in Jesse's arms. The harsh breathing stopped and Mallinson's head lolled to one side.

Jesse laid the body down and rose to his feet, finding himself trembling.

"You sure won't be needing no doctor now, mister," he breathed. He ran a big calloused hand across his own, suddenly dry lips.

"Where could he have come from, Jess?" Meg asked, white-faced. "And those scars on his back?"

"Mebbe we'll never know." He eyed the wrapped object Mallinson had given him then dropped it, unopened, on to the table. "I'll get him out to the barn an' in the morning take him to town. Mebbe the sheriff'll have an answer."

In the purpling light that rolled down from the Sierra Nevadas and spread itself across Jesse Fuller's wheat fields, the farmer carried Mallinson out to the barn, wrapped him in an old horse blanket and laid him in the back of the wagon.

Meg had lit the lamps and was waiting by the table staring down at the object as he returned. She looked up as Jesse joined her.

"Must have been real important from the way he carried it. What do you think it is, Jess?"

"Ain't but one way to find out," Jesse said, and carefully unwrapped the object, pulling away the fabric until before their startled eyes lay a triangular-shaped pendant of pure gold studded with diamonds and rubies attached to a gold chain.

* * *

"It's a puzzle boys an' no mistake. Have you ever heard of Cordoba's Treasure?" The elderly man spoke through a grey cloud of cigar smoke, fierce dark eyes regarding the two young men before him. The three were gathered in a tiny office at the rear of Midwest Freight Lines, Tucson.

Lounging against the wall by the window that looked out on to the freight yard, Wes Hardiman shrugged his lips. An inch or so under six foot, dark hair curling about his head, he had a pleasant, smiling face that was dominated by a pair of piercing, blue eyes. Powerfully built and clad in levis and a chestnut-brown hide coat over a blue shirt, a tied-down, single-action Colt Peacemaker hung comfortably on his right hip.

"Can't say I have, Colonel." His blue eyes drifted to his companion sprawled in a chair. His long legs were thrust out before him, crossed at the ankles. "You, Ben?"

Even sitting down, Ben Travis commanded respect. He was a big man. Standing he topped the six foot six mark, a good head taller than his companion and half as wide again. Clad from head to foot in light tan buckskin, a red bandanna adding a splash of colour at his throat, his broad, handsome face was topped with a mane of thick, silver hair. On his right hip he carried a British made, double-action Adams revolver that had been used extensively on both sides during the Civil War. On his left hip, encased in an ornate, Indian-crafted sheath, lay a broad-bladed Bowie knife.

Ben shook his head.

"That's a new one on me."

Both men settled their eyes on the older man and waited for an explanation.

Colonel Tom Paxton, retired, now ran the Midwest Freight Line, a legitimate concern that hid a less-publicized activity. The three were government agents, assignments coming through Paxton.

The colonel removed the cigar from his mouth. In his early fifties, he still retained a slim, whipcord body beneath the grey business suit. A leg injury had left him with a limp and put an end to an active army career. He had been destined for a desk job when the offer to head a small, covert section of men to handle internal problems, had been made. That had been six years and many successful assignments ago. The two before him were his top field agents.

He cleared his throat.

"Happen you boys'll need to be acquainted with a little history for this one. It was back in 1769 that a fella by the name of Jose de Galvez organized an expedition to colonize California; he wanted to show his Spanish superiors that he was doing his job. They already had a number of military garrisons set up in San Diego, San Francisco, Santa Barbara and Monterey and a few established, civilian towns, San Jose, Santa Cruz and Los Angeles, but they wanted more. The military leader of the expedition was Captain Gaspar de Portola an' with them were a group of Franciscan monks under the leadership of Father Junipero Serra."

"Sure are fancy names," Ben commented dryly.

"Besides a show of military and religious strength," Paxton continued, eyeing Ben, "they took with them a vast treasure. Gold, precious stones, jewellery. Guess they figured that if'n they couldn't defeat or convert they could buy."

"Them boys sure had all the angles covered," Wes spoke up.

"Except one." Paxton took a puff of his cigar.

"How's that, Colonel?" Ben asked curiously.

"Greed from within their own ranks. It came in the name of one Hernando de Cordoba, one of Portola's officers. Seems that one night, along with a group of like-minded friends, Hernando helped himself to a big chunk of treasure and high-tailed it into the hills. Story goes that he went up into the Sierra Nevadas and was never seen again. Him, his boys an' the treasure vanished. Belief is that they perished trying to get across the mountains an' so was born the legend of Cordoba's Treasure. A lost fortune waiting to be found."

"Maybe this Hernando fella was a lot smarter than they thought," Wes commented. "If'n they never found no bodies mebbe he got clean away with his treasure."

"Which means there ain't no treasure, only a legend," Ben added shrewdly.

"Well if'n he did, he never sold it. It never turned up, nor did Hernando de Cordoba or his men," Paxton said mildly.

"I get the feeling there's a punchline to this," Wes said.

"One helluva one," Paxton admitted. "Four months ago Senator James Meachen's son, Glen, went missing in the Sierra Nevadas. Word came down an' I sent a couple of our boys out to try an' find out what happened to him. I didn't hear anything from them until a month ago when a near dead man, half starved and practically naked appeared at a homesteader's door. He was pretty far gone according to reports an' he died not long after. He lived long enough to tell the homesteaders, Meg and Jesse Fuller, his name." Paxton paused. "It was Ray Mallinson."

"Our Ray Mallinson?" Ben cried.

"He was partnering Pete Mullins an' as yet, Pete hasn't been seen. Seems that Ray had been whipped pretty bad. He was carrying a bundle that he gave to the Fullers before he died. The bundle contained a gold necklace studded with diamonds. The Fullers took the body an' the necklace into Dry Ridge an' turned them both over to Sheriff Roy Cates. Cates sent the necklace to the Marshal's office in Carson City who in turn handed it over to the experts in Seattle." He paused for breath.

"Quite a journey it's bin having," Ben commented.

"The news finally came through this morning. The necklace has been positively identified as part of Cordoba's Treasure."

"They can be that sure?" Wes raised an eyebrow.

"Apparently so. Seems this Portola kept detailed records of the treasure they carried an' provided an equally detailed one of the items stolen by Cordoba. A number of copies were circulated at the time an' that's how we have one. Treasure-hunters have spent the last hundred years looking for it without luck, until now."

"So how did Ray get hold of it?" Wes asked.

"That's for you boys to find out, along with what happened to him, his partner an' the senator's son. Dry Ridge looks to be the place to start."

"An' jus' where is Dry Ridge?" Ben asked.

"It's a town on the California-Nevada border. If'n you take the overnight train to Carson City you could be in Dry Ridge by tomorrow night."

"Have we got a reason for being in Dry Ridge?" Wes asked, as Ben unfolded himself from the chair.

"You're agents for Midwest Freight looking to open up a line across the Sierra Nevadas. It'll give you a reason to poke about in the mountains without anyone getting suspicious."

"Hell, we'll be almost respectable for once," Ben breathed. Normally assignments meant them arriving at towns as drifters or travelling cow-punchers.

"There is a kicker to this," Paxton said. They had started for the door and his words stopped them in their tracks. Wes threw Ben a resigned look before settling his gaze on Paxton. "Cordoba's Treasure is reputed to be cursed. Seems that it contained a number of religious artefacts an' the priests didn't cotton to them being stolen, so they put a curse on it an' anyone who touches it."

"How'd you feel 'bout curses, Ben?" Wes asked, as they stepped out into Tucson's long Main Street.

"I've handled 'em before," Ben said matter-of-factly, causing Wes to throw him a surprised look.

"You have?" Wes blurted.

"Sure." A sudden twinkle came into Ben's eyes. "Warm beer and cold-hearted women, two of the worst curses a man ever had to face."

* * *

The Sierra Nevada mountains form a thick backbone that runs for 400 miles down the centre of California. Most of the range lies in California, but there is a small section that reaches into Nevada. It is here on the border where the two states meet in a broken, arid, dun-coloured landscape peppered with scrub and mesquite and stands of scruboak, that the town of Dry Ridge rises from the foothills of the towering range. A collection of tired, sun-dried buildings of weathered clapboarding and white adobe gathered either side of a wide street.

Wes and Ben rode into town to the ring of a blacksmith's hammer and headed for the saloon. Night was coming. The sun had already dipped beneath the high, granite crags filling the eastern face with deep, spreading shadows. It had been a long, tiring journey for them, first by train and then horseback and Ben was looking forward to a cooling beer or two. Beer was Ben's favourite drink. As they tied up outside the saloon, Ben's mind was on a foam-headed tankard, he failed to see what brought a frown to Wes's face.

With the coming of darkness, the stores up and down the street were closing rapidly. Normally they stayed open a lot longer, but here the owners seemed in a hurry to close and get away before the full onset of night. The few people there were on the street hurried to get back to their homes. One or two cast fearful glances in their direction and then were gone. In the silence of the lengthening shadows, Wes could sense an atmosphere. Apart from the sounds of occasional, raucous laughter coming from the saloon, the town had a depressing silence that grated on Wes's nerves.

Ben seemed impervious to the

atmosphere as he faced the saloon, a wedge of orange light washing over him coming from the establishment. He smiled in anticipation and licked dry, dusty lips.

"The first one ain't gonna touch the sides," he announced, and marched straight for the batwings. Wes shook his head and followed his big partner.

There were half a dozen men bellied against the long bar accompanied by a trio of gaudily clad, brassy-faced women. The men had been talking loudly, now all conversation ceased as they turned their eyes on the newcomers and an unnatural silence filled the saloon. If Ben noticed the silent stares he did not show it. He marched up to the bar and called over the nervous looking barkeep.

"Two of your coldest beers, fella, got me a desert in the throat that'll take some clearing." He smiled broadly and let his dark eyes drift around the sea of empty tables. "Business is slack tonight," he observed.

"It'll pick up later on," the barkeep said. He was a thin-faced, narrow-shouldered individual, dark hair slicked back over his head. Wes noticed the man's nervousness and it made him tense. Something was definitely not right about Dry Ridge.

2

"AIN'T exactly a welcoming place," Ben said softly to Wes as the two selected a table away from the bar and dropped down on to hard, uncomfortable chairs. "Kinda quiet."

"Kinda," Wes agreed. "I wonder why?"

"I hope it ain't the beer," Ben said, with a sudden worried look. He took a huge gulp of his tankard that reduced the contents to half and left a foam moustache on his upper lip. "No, it ain't that." There was a note of relief in his voice that brought a smile to Wes's face. He took a more refined sip of his own beer as a man detached himself from the bar and moved towards them. He was a big-bellied individual, clad in dark pants with a leather vest open over a dirty undershirt.

Lank, dark hair hung about his ears in thin, greasy locks.

"Well, lookee here, you boys got business in Dry Ridge?" He came to a halt before them and hooked thumbs in a gunbelt. The lower half of his fleshy face was dark with beard shadow. An insolent grin split lips over tobacco-stained teeth.

"Mebbe," Wes said, putting the glass down and resting both hands lightly on the table top before him.

"Mebbe ain't good 'nough, boy. You ain't got business then you must be drifters, saddle bums, an' we don' cotton to the likes of such no-accounts here."

"You could have fooled me," Ben spoke up.

The grin on the man's face faltered. "How's that again, boy?" he demanded.

"We got business," Wes cut in, giving Ben a warning glance.

"An' jus' what might that be?"

"Who's asking?" Ben cut in, earning himself a second glance from Wes.

Wes had caught the belligerent edge to Ben's voice and it surprised him. It took a lot to anger Ben, but this jasper had managed it in a few short minutes. It seemed that he was deliberately goading the two and Wes smelt a set-up. He cast a wary eye at the men at the bar. They had their backs to it, taut smiles on their hard faces, hands not far from their guns.

Ben's question broadened the smile on the man's face as though he had been waiting for the question.

"I'm asking, boy." As he spoke he flipped the vest aside on the left to reveal a star pinned over his heart. "Sheriff Lyle Rance and them's" — he jerked a thumb over his shoulder — "are my deputies." He hooked his thumb back in his gunbelt as the two exchanged startled glances.

"I thought Roy Gates was sheriff here?" Ben blurted out before he could stop himself and instantly the smile froze on Lyle's face.

"How come you know Gates?" he

demanded suspiciously.

"We passed through here a piece ago on business for the Midwest Freight Company an' met him then," Wes lied glibly.

"That's the truth of it, Sheriff," Ben agreed quickly.

The answer seemed to satisfy Lyle as he relaxed.

"Well ol' Roy, he done retired," Lyle declared. "Ain't that right, boys?" He called the last over his shoulder.

"S'right, Sheriff," came a chorus of agreement.

"Now think, you boys'ud better talk. Saddle bums git to taste the hospitality of the jail on account as they ain't tolerated in Dry Ridge. The last one couldn't hold his likker an' shot one of our good citizens. Cain't have that happening again, now kin we?"

"We're not here to make trouble, Sheriff," Wes said, in a placatory fashion. "My name's Wes Hardiman and this here's Ben Travis. We work for the Midwest Freight Company of

Tucson. We're here to see if'n it's possible to open a freight line across the mountains an' mebbe an office here."

"Well it ain't," Lyle said bluntly. "Reckon you boys've hadda wasted journey. Best get yourselves back to Tucson."

"Can't do that, Sheriff," Wes said blandly, but a hardness had settled in his eyes. "Gotta see for ourselves, company rules."

"I make the rules in Dry Ridge, boy, an' I say you an' your pardner ride out."

"And if'n we don't?" Wes challenged quietly, steel in his voice.

The grin faltered on the sheriff's face as he found two pairs of flinty eyes boring unflinchingly into him. He ran a nervous hand over his bristly chin. No one had ever faced him down like this before and he was at a loss as to what to do next. He threw a quick look at the group by the bar. They had turned their backs on him and gone back to drinking. He was on his own and that didn't sit too well with him.

"I'll be keeping a close eye on you boys an' if'n you step outa line I'll be there," he threatened lamely and turned away.

"What was all that about, d'yer think?" Ben side-mouthed across to Wes while keeping his eyes on Rance who had joined the men at the bar.

"Must be the local welcoming committee," Wes replied. His eyes too were on the sheriff who appeared to be having a heated exchange with the men.

"Reckon he needs to work on his welcoming speech a tad more," Ben said drily. His eyes flickered on to Wes. "If'n that boy's a duly elected lawman, then I'll eat my hoss, saddle an' all."

"That's my way of thinking too," Wes agreed. "Did you notice how quiet the town was when we arrived? Folks putting up the shutters an' high-tailing it."

"Same goes for this place," Ben said.

"A half-dozen customers an' they look like they're squirming to be away."

Wes let his eyes glide over the few solitary seated clientele dotted about the room.

"Something's going on here an' I don't like the feel of it." His eyes came to rest on the nearest drinker. Unaware that he was being watched the man raised his eyes to the big clock over the bar; it was almost eight. In a quick, jerky movement the man tossed the amber contents of his glass down his throat, rose to his feet, chair scraping, and hurried towards the batwings and the night beyond.

The others were rising to quickly follow the man. Eyes were cast at Wes and Ben, the glances quick and fearful. The only ones now remaining were the sheriff and his pards.

Ben lowered his almost empty tankard and threw Wes a quizzical look.

"I don't get this. The town's running scared, why?"

Wes cocked an ear. Muted, but

growing louder, came the clatter of hoofs mingled with crunch and ring of metal-rimmed wagon wheels.

"Mebbe we'll find out," Wes said.

Shots echoed from the street beyond mingled with the laughter of men and the sounds of voices. Wes eyed the sheriff. The man's head was turned towards the batwings, he was smiling. He glanced in their direction and his smile broadened. He said something to the other men and smiling faces peered at Wes and Ben.

Feet stamped the boardwalk outside and the next second men began filing into the saloon in a noisy crush. Wes estimated fifteen to twenty men. The human tide hit the bar and spread itself along its length calling loudly to the barkeep for service. The man slammed down glasses and three full bottles in a hurry and let grabbing hands do the rest.

A pianist in a gaudy vest and round-topped derby appeared and music filled the saloon. With happy squeals half a dozen silk-dressed girls trooped down the stairs from the upper region of the saloon to join the men. The two seated friends viewed it all in slack-jawed amazement. In a few seconds the drab, silent saloon had been transformed.

Bawdy cries filled the air and cigar smoke began to curl languidly about the ceiling-hung oil lamps. A few eyes had been cast in their direction, but for the most Wes and Ben had been ignored as more thirsty needs were catered for.

Sheriff Rance greeted the newcomers like old friends and a while later Wes observed him in conversation with a thickset, redheaded man. Both looked towards him and Ben and there were smiles and nods.

Wes felt a tense expectancy settle over him. When the two had broken apart Wes watched the red-haired man move across to a huge, bull of man whose shoulder width occupied an area taken up by two normal men.

"I think we've got trouble," Wes

whispered across to Ben. "The sheriffs been spouting a piece to the redhead, now the redhead's talking to the man mountain."

"Sure is a big ol boy," Ben agreed, as the big man and the redhead broke away from the bar and came towards the two. Others at the bar turned to watch and Wes glimpsed an evil smile on the sheriff's face.

Conversation died, only the piano player kept going, then he, too, stopped and silence filled the room.

"Good evening to yers, boys, an' a foine one it is to be sure." The redhead spoke with a thick, Irish brogue and his face wore a friendly smile. "The name's Mahonney, Patrick Mahonney, but most call me Red on account of the hair."

"I can see they would," Wes said and, after introducing Ben and himself, said, "What's your grievance, Red?"

Red threw back his head and laughed.

"To be sure and why would I have

a grievance against two such foine boys as yourselves?" His smile faded. "But my friend Ox here" — he gave Ox a slap on the back — "feels that you have offended him. I tried to explain that you being strangers in town did not mean to upset him, but once he gets a notion . . . " Red shrugged.

Wes eyed the silent Ox. The man was awesomely big, his wide shoulders clad in a red check shirt that hung open over a huge barrel of a belly. The light shone on his bald head and thickly jowled cheeks. Small, dark eyes in a brutish face glared at Wes. Although he was fat he exuded power and strength.

"So, what's his grievance?" Wes asked.

"You're sitting at my table." Ox spoke with a deep, rasping voice.

"A man of few words," Red sighed, "but succinctly put."

"Does he know any more or is that it?" Any hopes Wes had of trying to talk his way out of any possible trouble were dashed by Ben's words. Wes threw his partner a look that said whose side are you on? and tried to save the situation.

"Well, we were just about to leave an' Ox can have his table an' a drink on us to make up for upsetting him."

"Didn't I tell you, Ox, they didn't mean it." He glanced at Wes. "But 'tis not as simple as that." He almost sounded regretful.

"Didn't think it would be," Wes said flatly. He glimpsed the sheriff's grinning features. The man had set them up to get even for his own inadequacies.

"Ox is a simple soul. A challenge, me buckos. Ox here is the champion arm wrestler of all Nevada and California; 'tis yet to be found a man to beat him." Red's grin widened. "Now which of you shall take up the challenge?"

"Mebbe neither of us," Wes replied, causing Red to shake his head solemnly.

"T'would be a bad move not to accept, gentlemen. Ox would take it as a personal affront and then things would get ugly. Ox has a habit of breaking people's most treasured possessions like their arms or legs."

"Since you put it so nicely." Wes began dryly, only to have Ben cut in.

"What do we get for winning?"

"You can leave town in one piece."

"Heads you win, tails we lose," Ben mused. He looked at Wes. "Move aside, short fella, the big boys are gonna play."

Tight-lipped, Wes rose to his feet and moved to one side. Ox dragged a chair forward and sat himself down opposite Ben.

"There is just a little addition to make it more interesting," Red said. "Shorty!" A thin, weasel-faced man detached himself from the bar and scurried forward, handing something to Red. Smiling, the Irishman placed two objects on either side of the table and a wash of cold horror swept through Wes. The objects were blocks of wood, each with half a dozen fence nails hammered through them with a good inch of point showing. Placed as they were the loser would end up with a hand skewered to the block.

Wes threw Red a look.

"Now hold on." He took a step forward and felt the cold muzzle of a gun pushed into the back of his neck and heard the ratchet clicking of a hammer being thumbed back.

"One more step, mister, an' I'll blow your goddamned head off," a gravelly voice promised.

Wes had not been aware of anyone moving into position behind him, but from the corner of one eye he counted three shadowy forms spreading to his left. Others from the bar had moved forward, jostling for position in a semi-circle behind Ox.

"Best you be quiet now, Wes, the boys don't like to have their fun spoilt," Red said mildly.

Ben looked around and gave Wes a taut smile.

"Nothing to worry 'bout, pardner,

kinda makes it more interesting." He settled his eyes on Ox's fat, sullen face. "Ready when you are, lard barrel." He placed his right elbow on the table, hand in the air.

Ox glared at him as he placed his own beefy elbow on the table and hands were gripped.

"I'm gonna enjoy this," he rasped, and pulled back lips in a smile to reveal a set of broken, blackened teeth.

"Are we set, gentlemen?" Red enquired. "Then let battle commence."

Silence filled the saloon as the two locked muscles and began to push against each other. At first it seemed as though the two had been frozen into immobility. Neither man moved. Ox's face reddened with strain and the chair beneath him creaked. Ben's face was set hard, lips tightly compressed; only a slight flaring of the nostrils indicated the tension he was under.

Tendon and sinew creaked audibly as muscles strained and then slowly, to Wes's consternation, Ben's arm began to inch backwards. Ox leaned his body to one side to add weight to his pushing arm.

Ben's face had reddened beneath the tan and he compressed his lips in a tight, thin line, cheek muscles taut. A murmur ran through the watching crowd as Ben's hand was pushed closer to the waiting nails. They had seen it all before. Ox was unbeatable and, very soon, screams would ring out as Ox transfixed his opponent's hand to the block, for Ox never accepted surrender, he liked to maim.

Wes was tense as he stood there, eyes glued on the pair, temporarily forgetting the gun barrel pressed to his neck as he tried to will strength into his friend's arm.

"You're a tolerably strong man, Ox, reckon you win," Ben grunted, but Ox shook his head.

"I ain't heard you sing yet," he rasped, and continued to apply pressure.

Ben's eyes narrowed and became hard, granite chips. The downward travel of the knuckle whitened, locked hands came to a halt and then a gasp went up from the crowd as they witnessed the impossible. The big stranger was fighting back, forcing Ox's arm up.

Higher, higher until the arms were once more in the upright position and now it was Ox's arm that was being forced back and down towards the block.

Sweat flowed down Ox's face as a murmur of disbelief ran through the crowd and panic rode in his small, dark eyes. He breathed harshly through flaring nostrils as the back of his hand was pushed relentlessly towards the gleaming nail points.

At the last moment Ben swept the block aside with his other hand and slammed Ox's hand down hard on the table top.

"You'd better give thanks to the good Lord that I was in a good mood, fat boy," Ben grated and released his grip.

Ox sat back nursing his numb hand and eyeing Ben with undisguised hatred as uproar broke out in the saloon.

"Bejesus!" Red Mahonney's jaw had dropped and while some of the men, grinning broadly, took their rewards for bets unexpectedly won, most looked surprised for they had witnessed the impossible.

"Yep, just tolerably strong," Ben mused, loud enough for Ox to hear. The fat man rose to his feet and lumbered to the bar, shouldering aside anyone unfortunate enough to be in the path. He grabbed up a bottle and with a final, murderous glare at Ben, stalked from the saloon.

"Now there's a sight I never expected to see," Red said ruefully, eyeing Ben with some admiration. "'Tis a bad enemy you made this night, Mr Ben Travis, an' that's for sure."

"I don't figure to lose much sleep over it," Ben replied.

A smile flickered up the corners

of Red's mouth but did not reach his eyes.

"Maybe it is you should," he said grimly. "Only one man has ever beaten Ox before."

"Well now there's two of us," Ben pointed out, and Red shook his head.

"Only you, me bucko, for was not the other fella found the very next day with his neck broke and no one sure how it happened? Accident they said." Red smiled engagingly.

"Happen I'll remember that," Ben promised.

"Happen you will, my big friend, but if I was you I'd be looking for someplace where accidents don't happen."

"If'n I was you I guess I would, but I'm not and here suits me real fine." Ben returned the smile. Red dipped his head and turned away, joining the other men who were drifting back to the bar now the excitement was over.

The one who had held the gun on Wes had reholstered his weapon and was walking to join his pards when Wes called out, "Hold on, mister." The man paused and turned to Wes, eyes enquiring. The next second a fist that had the feel of a mule kick landed on the underside of his jaw. The man's feet left the floor and he flew backwards overturning a table and scattering two chairs before coming to rest in a sprawled heap on the wooden floor. Wes stood over him. "Don't ever pull a gun on me again, mister, unless you're prepared to use it," he warned the barely conscious man.

A rattle of gun hammers being pulled back snapped Wes's head up and he found himself looking down the barrel of a Colt .45.

3

SHERIFF LYLE RANCE grinned over the barrel of the gun. Flanked by his henchmen, who had refused earlier to back his play, Ben also found himself covered.

"I'll use it, boy, if'n you make a move for that hogleg. Like I said we don' 'preciate drifters getting likkered up an' causing trouble. Got jist the place for the likes o' you," Lyle crowed.

"Now hold on, Sheriff," Wes began, as the cowboy he had assaulted scrambled to his feet and staggered groggily to the bar.

"Boy, you keep argifying wi' the law an' you could end up a permanent resident o' Dry Ridge, now unbuckle the bunbelts an' let 'em drop, real easy like. Don' try anythin' fancy; the boys have got mighty nervous fingers, if'n you catch my drift?"

"We do, Sheriff," Ben intervened, keeping his hand well away from his Adams, as he moved lightly to Wes's side. He eyed his partner's set, angry face. "Best do as the man says, Wes. It's a mite difficult to make a complaint from a coffin." To match his words Ben unbuckled his gunbelt and let it drop to the floor.

"Your friend's showing sense, boy," Lyle smirked.

Wes glared darkly at the sheriff, but to Ben's relief let his gunbelt drop.

"You just made one hell of a mistake, Rance," he said coldly.

"Depends how you look at it, boy. These boys work for Thad Tolver out at the Circle T ranch. Reckon he ain't gonna take too kindly to a couple o' drifters beating up on his cowhands. 'Sides, I ain't the one on the wrong end of a gun. Now move."

* * *

Dry Ridge jail consisted of two, cage-fronted cells in a room at the rear of the sheriffs once. Side by side the two six by eight cells shared a narrow, horizontal opening that served as a window high on the rear wall below which a pair of rough, wooden bunks offered the prospect of little comfort. A pair of lidded slop buckets concluded the amenities. Outside the cells a single, ceiling-hung oil lamp threw the shadows of the bars over the two men.

Wes stared about dismally and prodded the straw-filled sack that served as a mattress with a grimace of distaste, then a rueful grin flickered across his face as he peered through the side bars at Ben in the next cell.

"We were looking for accommodation for the night."

"Sure was kind of the sheriff to put us up free of charge," Ben returned dryly, as he sat gingerly on the end of his bunk nearest the central dividing bars. It creaked and groaned, but held his weight. Both could hear the muted sound of music and laughter together with the occasional girlish shriek coming from the saloon.

"What do you figure's going on here, Wes?"

"I don't know, big fella, but I'm sure itching to find out." Wes sat on the end of his bunk, half turned to face Ben through the bars. He held out a hand and began ticking off points as he spoke. "So far we've found out that strangers aren't welcome in Dry Ridge, the townsfolk are running scared and I'm pretty sure that something has happened to Roy Cates, the real sheriff of Dry Ridge. Rance is working for someone else an' it's my guess that someone is going to turn out to be this Thad Tolver of the Circle T."

"He sure seemed on friendly terms with Red an' his boys," Ben agreed, "and I'll tell you something else. If'n them fellas are cowboys then I'm the back end of a cow."

Wes eyed his partner strangely.

"What makes you say that?"

"Fella rides the range an' it leaves its mark on him, the weather gets burned into his skin, palms of the hands get ridged and hard from gripping the reins. Fella gets a peculiar way of walking that comes from spending days in the saddle. Red an' his boys ain't got none of those things. Ox now, his palms were hard and calloused all over. I saw the same in Red's hands, an more'n half of them wore lace-up boots, thick and heavy, not the sort of boot a genuine cowboy would wear."

"A Saturday-night-out boot?" Wes suggested, and Ben smiled.

"Them boots were well worn, the type of wear that only comes from daily use, all day an' every day. I'd say they don't sit a horse to make a living."

Wes eyed his partner. Ben was a shrewd observer of people and now he had voiced his observations something that had been niggling at Wes came to the surface. The clothes worn by Red and his boys were not quite right; not exactly cowboy-style, they looked more like . . . Ben was smiling at Wes.

"Are you thinking what I'm thinking?" he prompted.

"Miners?" Wes ventured cautiously.

"On the button," Ben agreed. "Them boys'ud be more at home chasing gophers than cattle. So what's a cattleman doing hiring a bunch of miners?"

"What indeed?" Wes mused thoughtfully.

* * *

"Wake up, boys, rise an' shine, it's chow time." The wheezing voice had them awake in an instant. Daylight filtered through the window slit. Wes swung his feet to the ground. His body clock plus the chill in the air told him that it was just after dawn. He yawned and stretched his arms before focussing his attention on the short figure the other side of the bars.

He was clad in an assortment of shabby, ill-fitting garments that were either a size too large or a size too small; garments that had been well worn and then discarded, but in him were finding a new lease of life. The clothes were topped off by an old hat that looked like a pack-rat had used it as a nest. The face beneath the hat was decorated with bushy, grey and white whiskers. Between the whiskers and the flopping hat-brim a pair of bright, dark, button eyes peered from a surround of weathered, nut-brown skin. He clutched a wooden tray from which the aroma of coffee, hot and strong, reached out and tantalized the nostrils of both prisoners.

"Brunged yer breakfas', cornbread, beans an' coffee," announced the apparition. "Ah gits me a dollar each for feeding you boys, so the longer you stay here the richer I git. The name's Poke. Did have another one once, but I disremember it now." He pushed food and coffee through a tiny, rectangular opening in each door and stood back, eyeing the two.

Ben took a sip of his coffee and spluttered.

"Hell, Poke, what did you make this coffee out of, wood tar?"

"Gotta be strong, it's how I likes it. Hear you boys had a run in with Tolver's men." He eyed Ben. "Hear tell you whupped Ox arm wrestling; sure wished I'd seen that." Wes detected a wistful note in the oldster's voice and sensed a source of information at hand.

"How come the townsfolk were missing last night, Poke?"

"When Tolver's boys come to town it ain't fit for decent folk to be on the street. They's a mean bunch when they get likker into 'em an' that's for sure." He nodded to emphasize his words. "Mind you the meanest one you ain't met an' you wanna keep it that way. He's called Ace Reynolds, but he's known as The Ace of Spades, 'cause he always wears black an' the fact that if'n he draws his gun on a fella that fella's dead. He's a gunsel an' Tolver's right-hand man."

"We'll bear it in mind," Wes said.

"How come they don't like strangers here?" Ben asked.

Poke scratched his nose.

"Bin like that since Sheriff Cates left and Lyle Rance took over. Used to be a good town one time."

"What happened to Cates?" Wes asked.

"Him and Tolver didn't see eye to eye, then one day Cates is gone and Lyle's wearing a badge an' he takes orders from Tolver."

"Does this Tolver jasper run a mine?" Wes prodded.

"Hell no, young fella, he's a cattleman, biggest rancher hereabouts. Somethin' wrong with your beans?" He scowled at the pair who had put their plates aside. "Cornbread's a mite on the hard side, but if yer dunk it in yer coffee it'll soften up pretty quick."

"I'll sure remember that," Wes promised.

Just then the door leading to the outer office opened and Lyle Rance strutted in. He glared at Poke.

"What the hell you hanging 'bout here for, Poke? Get on out."

"Jus' going, Sheriff," Poke said quickly and scurried out.

Rance peered at the two.

"What's the old coot been saying?"

"Just giving us lessons in how to make the cornbread edible," Wes replied. "So how long are you holding us for, Rance?"

"Now that's a question," Rance drawled, pausing before the cells and massaging his stubbly chin with a grimy hand, eyes flicking from one to the other. "Causing a disturbance, resisting arrest." He dropped his hand to join the other one, thumb hooked in gunbelt, a smile on his flabby, unwashed face. "Reckon to add threatening a duly elected officer of the law an' you boys have got yourselves a whole passel of trouble."

"Now hold on, Sheriff!" Wes began hotly.

"Wouldn't surprise me none if'n there weren't dodgers out on you boys." Rance grinned nastily. "Reckon I'll have to put a wire out, check around, see if'n you're known criminals. Sure to take a time though. A week, mebbe more." Lyle Rance was enjoying himself and the shocked expressions the two displayed added to his enjoyment.

Wes threw his tin mug aside and it clattered across the stone floor. He stepped forward and gripped the bars in a knuckle-whitening hold.

"Damaging county property as well," Rance said, his eyes following the mug until it was still.

"Just wire Colonel Tom Paxton at the Midwest Freight offices, Tucson; he'll vouch for us."

"Ain't that simple, boy. This colonel fella is probably in cahoots with you. Why, he's likely to tell me you're good ol' boys, I let you free an' the next minute you're out robbing a bank. Gotta make real sure afore I let you out to mix with decent, honest folk."

"That's rubbish, Rance, and you know it."

"That's just it, boy, I don't know until I'm told different," Rance said, smiling.

"Who by, Tolver?" Wes said heatedly.

Rance's face darkened.

"Forget it, Wes. Reckon the sheriff's only doing his job," Ben cut in, earning himself a savage glare from Wes.

Rance's face cleared.

"Your partner's got the right idee, boy. You gotta co-operate with the law not sassy-mouth it," he said, not taking up on the name Wes had let slip.

"I'm sure you'll do your duty, Sheriff," Ben replied smoothly.

"That's the way of it," Rance agreed amiably. "Now you boys behave an' we'll get along real fine." Chuckling to himself, Rance sauntered out leaving the two alone.

Ben eyed his friend.

"Ain't like you to run off at the mouth, that's what I do."

A rueful smile chased the anger from Wes's face.

"I hate beans for breakfast," Wes replied, by way of explanation. "Guess we wait."

Ben took a mouthful of beans and grimaced.

"Hell, I hate beans for breakfast as well."

* * *

As events turned out, the pair did not have long to wait.

It was mid-morning. Sunlight angled in dusty bars through the front window of the sheriffs office and crossed the room in a series of diagonal slashes. Rance was about to take his first drink of the day when the door to the street burst open and a heavily built man of medium height entered. Clad in a grey, three-piece suit, a black stetson was jammed on a head of thick, white hair that tumbled to his collar. He marched purposefully to the desk and stopped, anger in his brown eyes.

"Mr Tolver!" There was more than a hint of panic in the slovenly sheriff's voice at the sight of his visitor. Rance tried to do a dozen things at once in his flustered panic and only succeeded in knocking the contents of his glass across the desk top.

"Drinking on the job again, Rance? I'm beginning to think I made a real big mistake in setting you up as sheriff," Tolver snarled angrily, eyes spitting fire. A white moustache curved about his upper lips offsetting the berry brown of his tanned features.

In his late thirties Thad Tolver had been a cowhand before he became a rancher and it still showed through the made-to-measure suit and hand-crafted boots. His beginnings may have been humble, but he had had dreams and the ability to turn those dreams into reality. His methods had been more than questionable; he had rustled his first herd of cattle and from there he had built an empire riding roughshod over any who opposed him. He had a reputation for being ruthless and that reputation was backed up by the tall, whipcord-thin man clad in black but for a white silk shirt under a black leather vest. He wore a pearl-handled Colt Lightning strapped low on his left thigh and while his right hand was hooked in his gunbelt his left hand hung close to the bolstered gun.

Rance swallowed several times before finding words.

"Purely medicinal, Mr Tolver," he quavered.

"You've got two men in jail I hear?" Tolver snapped.

"Yes, sir. Strangers; caused trouble so I had to jail 'em."

"You're a fool, Rance, and a drunk. I heard about last night's events an' it don't sit too well with me."

"But you said to get rid of any strangers that come to town. They didn't look to wanna go, so I figured a coupla days in jail would make up their minds," Rance defended.

"You figured wrong, Rance. Red told me their names. Wes Hardiman and Ben Travis are troubleshooters from the Midwest Freight Company. They can cause trouble an' that's the last thing I need."

"Well how was I to know?" Rance said miserably.

"You use your head," Tolver hissed. "Saddle bums and drifters you can get rid of how you like, but anyone else, you get word to me. Now, release 'em."

"Let 'em go?" Rance wailed.

"You heard Mr Tolver," the gunman spoke for the first time, his voice no more than a hoarse whisper, eyes flat and dead in his pale face.

Rance looked into the expressionless face and a shudder of fear washed through him. The man's whispering voice had been the result of being guest of honour at a necktie party in the distant past. Beneath the black bandanna he wore were the indelible marks of the rope that had damaged his larynx and had almost ended his life. It was that episode that had turned him into the brutal, deadly killer that he was.

Rance nodded and clambered to his feet.

"Right away, Mr Tolver, right away," he mumbled.

Unaware of what had happened in the outer office, the two prisoners showed surprise when a sullen-faced Rance entered and unlocked their cells.

"Out," he said. "You're free to go."

Wes eyed him warily as he stepped cautiously out of the cell. Anxious to be free, the suddenness of it made him suspicious.

"What game are you playing, Rance?" he asked icily.

"Ain't no game. Mr Tolver said to let you go."

"That's mighty big of him," Ben said. "How about you lead the way,

Rance? We wouldn't like your pals to think we were making a break for it and accidentally shoot us."

Rance glared at him.

"Ain't no trick," he muttered, as he walked forward to the door. As he passed Ben the big man stepped forward, neatly lifted the gun from his holster and pressed it against Rance's neck, thumbing the hammer.

"It ain't no trick," Rance squeaked, coming to a halt, sweat breaking out on his face.

"Just a little insurance," Ben said. "Now move!"

Thad Tolver was standing looking out of the window when the door to the cells opened and a white-faced Rance appeared. A brief smile touched the cattleman's face as he took in the situation.

"I see you are cautious men," he said.

"Helps a body stay alive a little longer," Ben agreed.

"I'm Thad Tolver. When I heard

about the sheriff's little mistake I came as quickly as I could. We have had trouble in town before with strangers and I'm afraid it's made Sheriff Rance a little over-eager in his duties."

"We all make little mistakes," Ben said affably and with a sudden movement slammed the barrel of the pistol against the side of Rance's head. The man went to his knees with a moan, catching hold of the edge of the desk to save from measuring his length on the floor. "Sorry, Sheriff," Ben said with mock apology. "Didn't see you there; my little mistake." He now held the gun on Tolver, seeing the black-clad Reynolds tense.

"It's all right, Mr Reynolds, Mr . . . is it Hardiman or Travis? is not going to do anything foolish."

"Travis, Ben Travis," Ben supplied.

"The man who beat Ox at his own game."

"So what brings you galloping to our rescue, Tolver?" Wes spoke for the first time.

"Just trying to smooth the wheels of injustice. You can put up the gun, Mr Travis, I am not here to harm you or your partner.

Ben eyed him and then with a shrug angled the gun at the ceiling and lowered the hammer. Ace Reynolds' hand hardly seemed to move but Ben found himself looking down the barrel of the Colt Lightning above which a pair of flat, emotionless dark eyes stared unblinkingly at him from an unreadable face.

4

A TRICKLE of icy fear ran down Ben's spine as he stood frozen to the spot, pistol angled uselessly at the ceiling. Beside him Wes hardly dared to breathe.

A wagon rattled by outside; a fly buzzed in one corner of the dirty window, its wings sending sparkling dust motes into the air. Even Rance ceased struggling to haul himself to his feet and stare with dazed eyes at Reynolds. It was a moment frozen in time.

"OK, gentlemen, we've shown our teeth, so to speak. Put up your weapons and we can get on with the business in hand." Tolver spoke briskly and the moment passed. "If someone would be kind enough to assist the sheriff to a chair?"

Ben, keeping an eye on Reynolds,

lowered the gun and tossed it on to the desk top, forcing himself to relax.

"Sure, why not." He slid his hands under Rance's armpits and hauled the man up effortlessly and dumped him in the chair behind the desk. "There you go, ol fella," he said soothingly. "Don't go running your head into any gun barrels again."

Rance, still dazed, nodded uncomprehendingly.

"What business?" Wes asked, as Ben straightened from his task and gave the black-clad gunman a hooded glance. Reynolds stood with thumbs hooked in his gunbelt, gun back in its well-oiled holster.

Tolver's eyes travelled to some wooden pegs above where Rance sat lolling.

"I believe those gunbelts are yours, gentlemen? Feel at liberty to wear them now, I'm sure it'll ease your minds." He beamed like a favourite uncle visiting with candles. As Ben tossed Wes's gunbelt across, he lip-shrugged at the smaller man as if to say, what the hell's going on? Tolver's eyes fell on Ben's gun. "I see you favour a British made Adams, Mr Travis. An admirable weapon; proved itself in the war between the states on both sides. I used one myself at that time." His eyes settled on Wes. "The business, Mr Hardiman, is getting this little misunderstanding sorted out to everyone's mutual satisfaction."

"I'll go along with that," Wes agreed.

"Excellent," Tolver said with a smile. "You two have a reputation for being reasonable men and I can see it is true."

"We do?" Wes said with a narrowing of eyes. "And how would you know that?"

"No mystery, Mr Hardiman. I used Midwest Freight a couple of years ago. The drivers used to stay over at the ranch and I got to hear some of the bunkhouse stories they told about the pair of you in establishing new freight trails. I'm given to understand that's what you are in Dry Ridge for?"

"We're looking into the possibility of a freight trail over the mountains. If there is one that's suitable we will be setting up an office here," Wes admitted.

Tolver nodded.

"I wish you luck, but if there was such a trail I would have found it long ago."

"We'll take a look now that we're here."

"Of course, I would expect nothing less of you. In the meantime, while you are here, I have taken the liberty of acquiring two rooms at the Ridge Hotel for the duration of your stay. They are on me; it's the least I can do to make amends for our sheriff's over-eagerness."

"Well that's mighty fine of you," Wes said.

"The least I can do," Tolver repeated. "Your horses are over in the livery and anything you want, just call on me, any time. In fact," — he paused — "yes, I'm throwing a little celebration for my birthday next Saturday and I'd like the pair of you to attend and perhaps we can discuss your progress?"

"I'm sure we'll be able to make it," Wes said.

"Good, good." Tolver seemed genuinely pleased.

"The Circle T's not hard to find. Take the west trail out of town and it's about twenty miles." Tolver smiled happily. He was still smiling as Wes and Ben left the Sheriff's office, but once the door closed on the two, the smile faded.

Thad Tolver rounded on Rance who, apart from suffering a headache, had now recovered.

"You have one chance to redeem yourself, Rance. I want those two watched like a hawk. I want to know where they go, who they speak to and what they do. Fail me on this and Mr Reynolds will be paying you a call. Do I make myself clear?"

Rance nodded unhappily. "What if'n they leave town?"

"That will be taken care of. You concentrate on what happens in town."

"I won't fail, Mr Tolver," Rance promised, not liking the cold, deadly half-smile that had appeared on Reynolds' face.

"I'm glad to hear it," Tolver said, turned away and marched out of the office.

Ace Reynolds lingered in the doorway looking back at Rance.

"Be seeing you real soon, Sheriff," he whispered, and followed Tolver out.

* * *

"What do you make of Tolver, Wes?" Ben asked, as they angled across the wide, rutted street to where a sign over a doorway read Ridge Hotel in red letters.

"An honest man don't need the likes of Ace Reynolds at his side."

"That's a fact," Ben agreed with a

shiver as they paused on the sidewalk before the hotel entrance. "That fella's pure hell."

"He's got the so-called sheriff in his pocket which means he controls the town an' that makes me think that maybe the previous sheriff had a little lead persuasion to retire."

"You think Tolver had him killed?" Ben questioned in a low tone.

"Reckon him to have had a hand in Gates' retirement," Wes replied grimly.

"Why did he bother to spring us an' then go to the expense of providing hotel rooms for us?"

Wes looked serious.

"How it appears to me is that Rance did overstep the mark when he arrested us. Strangers are not wanted in Dry Ridge. The best way to get rid of them is to throw them in the calaboose for a couple of days. When they get out they'll be only too pleased to make tracks out of here. We, on the other hand, are a couple of ornery characters ready to raise a ruckus that could bring outside law snooping. Good ol' Thad knew that and he figured the best way to stop it was an up-front display of displeasure at Rance and free rooms for us as a sweetener. Hell, the way he invited us to his birthday party was a finishing touch of pure genius. No man's gonna kick up a ruckus after that."

"So what's he trying to cover up?"

"That, big fella, is the quesion. Come on let's get cleaned up and find a place to eat."

"There may be another reason for supplying the rooms," Ben said thoughtfully, stopping Wes in his tracks.

"How's that?"

"He knows exactly where we are and can keep an eye on us."

Wes gave his partner an admiring gaze.

"Hell, Ben, you're getting as devious as me in your thinking."

"Must be the company I keep," Ben replied with a smile as he followed Wes into the hotel lobby.

The desk clerk was all over them, fussing about as though they were kings from a foreign land. They were given two rooms at the front overlooking the main street. Wes was looking out when he saw Tolver and the black-clad gunman leave the sheriff's office.

His suspicions of the rancher were well founded as he drew a fresh shirt from his warbag. The shirt was not folded and rolled in exactly the same way he did it. The contents of the warbag were not in the same position he remembered. His belongings had been searched. Maybe Thad Tolver suspected something and needed proof, not that Wes was carrying anything to indicate his and Ben's real intention at Dry Ridge.

Wes smiled grimly to himself. If Ben was more than half right in that Tolver had given them the rooms to keep an eye on them, then maybe it could work to their advantage?

Later, refreshed, they ambled outside

to find a place to eat.

In the light of day Dry Ridge hummed and buzzed like any normal town, a far cry from the frightened silence of the previous night.

After eating they went across to the livery.

"Reckon old Poke might be able to answer a few questions if'n we put 'em right," Wes said, as they approached the livery.

"Might at that," Ben agreed. "He sure was a gabby cuss at the jail." But their expectations were not to be realized. They found Poke inside the big barn forking hay, but it was a different Poke to the one who had supplied their jail food. His left cheekbone sported a livid bruise that had reached up to colour his eyes.

"Dammit, Poke, what happened to you?" Wes cried, running his eyes over the old man's injuries.

"Tripped over a rake an' hit my head on the edge of the stall," Poke replied, avoiding Wes's eyes.

"Is that a fact?" Wes drawled thoughtfully, and the old man rounded on him.

"Can't a body trip over in his own goddam stable?" he demanded belligerently.

"Steady on, fella," Wes placated with a laugh. "We thought you might give us the lowdown on Dry Ridge an' some of the folks hereabouts."

"Well you thought wrong, son. I got work to do an' chawing the breeze with you boys ain't gonna get it done. Your horses are out back, bin fed an' watered, saddles are on the fence."

"That's real obliging of you, Poke. How much do we owe you?" Wes asked, not pushing the point.

"The boss said you wus to have everything free for as long as you're here," Poke answered, and Wes and Ben exchanged puzzled glances.

"You don't own this place, Poke?" Ben enquired and Poke smiled mirthlessly.

"Used'ta, then I hit a bad patch. Borrowed money from the bank then one day the bank called in my marker. I couldn't pay so Thad Tolver took over my marker an' now I work for him."

* * *

"Seems to me that someone persuaded ol' Poke that talking to us is not a healthy thing to do," Wes said, as later the two took the north-east trail out of town.

"Reckon they used a gun barrel to do the persuading with," Ben agreed grimly.

They were heading out to the Fuller spread to have a talk with Jesse and Meg Fuller. To the west, the ridge of the Sierra Nevadas dominated in a series of high, thrusting peaks, the lower slopes clothed in green. As they rode, the sand and brush gradually gave way to ever-growing patches of grass that finally knitted into a huge, lush plain that rose and fell in a series of gentle humps.

Some two hours after leaving Dry Ridge they spotted a log farmhouse surrounded by a collection of tall barns beyond which lay a vast sea of wheat. They rode up to the house and were about to dismount when a female voice called from the darkened, open doorway of the farmhouse.

"I'd be obliged if'n you stay on your horses, that way it makes it easier for you to turn around and off my property." The words were accompanied by an ominous ratchet clicking.

The two exchanged startled glances. Wes stared into the darkened opening where he could vaguely discern a standing figure.

"Excuse me, ma'am," Wes began.

"Maybe you think a woman can't shoot straight, or won't, but with this I don't have to and I will if'n I have to." The figure moved into the light to reveal a slim young woman clad in pants and a check shirt that did little to hide the feminine curves of her body. A rich fall of chestnut hair either side of her pretty face reached to her shoulders. Big hazel eyes that were more fitted to laughter than frowning, glared stonily at them.

Wes's eyes drifted to the ten gauge shot-gun held steadily in her slim hands.

"You surely don't, ma'am," he agreed, settling back in the saddle and tilting back his hat.

"Go back and tell Tolver the land is not for sale."

"Whoa down, ma'am. You're making a mistake, we don't work for Tolver," Wes said.

"Then what are you doing here?"

"We've come to speak to the Fullers," Ben cut in.

"You are," she said curtly. "I'm Mandy Fuller."

"It's Jesse and Meg we're here to see," Wes took over.

"That can be arranged if'n you don't get off my land." She spoke harshly, and there was a catch in her voice.

"I'm sorry, ma'am, I'm not catching your drift," Wes said, a puzzled frown on his face.

"They're both dead and if'n I could prove it was your boss Tolver who did it, he'd be in jail now." She waved the shot-gun. "Now get off my land or you'll be buried here."

Wes held up his hands.

"I'm sorry to hear that, Miss Fuller, we didn't know and, at the risk of repeating myself, we don't work for Tolver and from what we know of the man, ain't likely that we ever would. This here's Ben Travis and I'm Wes Hardiman and we work for the Midwest Freight Company out of Tucson looking to open a freight office in Dry Ridge." He maintained the lie out of caution.

For the first time doubt showed in her eyes.

"How do I know you're telling the truth?" she asked, still suspicious.

"Guess you'll have to take us at face value, ma'am," Wes replied levelly.

She eyed them keenly and the anger and aggression washed from her face leaving it tired and hollow-eyed. The shot-gun sagged in her hands and she fell back against the wall of the farmhouse, using it as a support.

Ben was off his horse in an instant, concern in his face as he darted to her side.

"Ma'am, are you all right?" he asked.

She turned her big hazel eyes on him, opened her mouth as though to speak, then the shot-gun slid from her hands and clattered to the floor of the porch, her eyes closed and she fell sideways. Ben caught her and hoisted her effortlessly in his arms.

"Dammit, Wes, she's passed out," Ben cried, turning to Wes.

"Must be the effect you have on women," Wes murmured. "Let's get her inside and comfortable and then find out what's going on here when she comes to."

5

MANDY FULLER opened her eyes and found herself stretched out on her own couch looking up at the parlour ceiling. For a second nothing registered. She heard male voices, pitched low, and smelt freshly made coffee. Panic seized her. She sat up in a sudden flurry that sent a wave of dizziness spinning through her head.

Chairs scraped and shapes loomed before her swimming eyes. She pressed herself back into the couch, terror starting in her eyes.

"Easy, ma'am, it's Wes and Ben." Wes crouched down before her, a friendly smile on his face and suddenly she remembered the two riders.

"What happened?" she asked.

"You passed out. Reckon it was the sight o' Ben's ugly mug," Wes joked.

"We made some coffee, ma'am, reckon you can stand a cup?" Ben called, from the table by the window.

"Yes please." She eyed Ben with some fascination, his silver hair and youthful, handsome face somehow at odds with each other, yet blending perfectly.

"How are you feeling, ma'am?" There was genuine concern in Wes's voice as he spoke and she gave him a wan smile as her earlier apprehension faded.

"Nothing that a little sleep won't put right and my name's Mandy." She flushed a little. "I must look a sight."

"Prettiest picture I've seen in a long while," Ben said gallantly, as he came across with a cup of coffee and handed it to her. She smiled gratefully up at him.

"Thank you, Mister . . . ?"

"Ben, ma'am." He beamed down at her.

She dropped her eyes to Wes.

"And you are Wes."
"On the button," Wes agreed.
"I remember now. How long have I been out?"
"Couple hours." Wes climbed to his feet.
"It was stupid of me."
"Reckon there was cause if'n Thad Tolver has anything to do with it." As he spoke Wes turned a chair around and sat on it facing her and Ben followed suit. "Care to tell us about it?"
She sipped her coffee and was silent for a moment.
"I came here from St Louis, where I was working as a schoolteacher, three weeks ago following the death, no, murder of my parents."
"What happened to them exactly?" Wes prompted gently.
"I don't really know, Wes," she said unhappily. "By the time the awful news reached me and I had made arrangements for the trip out here, they had been buried in the town

cemetery." She bit her lip and lowered her head as tears welled in her eyes.

Wes came to his feet in an instant.

"Please don' fret yourself, Mandy. I'm sorry to be stirring bad memories."

She lifted her head, running a hand across her reddened eyes, forcing a smile.

"I'm all right, really. According to that person who serves as sheriff in Dry Ridge . . ."

"Lyle Rance," Ben mumbled.

"You've met him then?"

"We've met," Wes said briefly. "Go on, Mandy."

"He said that Ma and Pa were killed by an outlaw gang, the Slaters, some four weeks earlier."

"That would put it mebbe a week after the man with the pendant showed up here," Wes murmured, as he reseated himself earning a curious glance from Mandy.

"How did you know about that?" she asked sharply, a little of her earlier apprehension returning. "It was in the last letter Ma sent me before she was killed."

"I'll tell you later," Wes promised. "Just how does Thad Tolver fit into all this?"

"He wants to buy the farm according to Ma's letters; he's been trying for years, but Pa would never sell up. I figure he thought I would be more inclined to sell."

"I take it he's approached you with an offer?" Wes said.

"If you can call it that," she said with a sniff. "It was well below the market value and I told him so. It's my inheritance, all I have left of my parents. I don't intend to sell this place and I told him so." She flushed defiantly.

"I guess that didn't make him too happy," Wes commented.

"You guess correctly. The fields are ready for harvesting, but suddenly there is no local labour able to help, and with the riders that come at night, — "

"How's that ma'am?" Ben demanded.

"They come at night and ride around in the darkness, calling out my name and laughing. I haven't slept for days. Of course I can't prove these riders are anything to do with Tolver, but it's too much of a coincidence otherwise." She passed a hand across her eyes as tears welled again and Wes saw a girl at the end of her tether. "I don't know how much more of this I can take."

A flinty gleam appeared in Ben's eyes. He hated to see folk put upon, females especially.

"Don't you concern yourself, little lady. I reckon Wes and I can give these riders a surprise. How 'bout it, Wes?"

Wes had seen this coming. On the one hand he wanted to help the girl but, on the other, he did not want to see their position compromised. He thought furiously for a second or two and an idea began to form that might be beneficial to both parties.

"There might be a way," he agreed cautiously.

"You'll help me?" The relief was apparent in her eyes.

"Reckon it could be of mutual benefit to both of us but, first of all, it means entrusting you with our real purpose here," he said gravely, and proceeded to tell her of the legendary Cordoba's Treasure, the missing men, and what had happened to them in town the night before.

"It's like that every Friday night in town when Tolver's men come in. The town shuts up and people keep out of the way." She smiled thinly. "The one thing I've learned since being here is that Tolver owns Dry Ridge."

"We sorta figured that," Ben said.

"What do you have in mind, Wes?" she asked.

"Well, for one thing it would mean Ben and I moving in here with you."

"That's no problem," she said quickly. "There's plenty of room."

"Might not do your reputation much good in the eyes of the townsfolk," Wes pointed out.

Her eyes flickered from one to the other and a roguish smile tugged at her lips chasing the worry from her eyes.

"Does a girl good to get talked about once in a while, but won't it make Tolver suspicious?"

"No more'n he is already. 'Sides we're here to open up a freight office and scout a trail across the mountains." He grinned boyishly from one to the other. "With your permission, ma'am, this here'd make a dandy freight office for the Midwest Freight Company."

A slow smile spread across Ben's face.

"Works for me, pardner," he agreed with a nod, but Mandy still had reservations.

"Will Tolver believe it?"

"He'll choke on it, but he'll believe it," Wes assured her. "The Midwest Freight Company is powerful enough to cause trouble if'n two of its men up and vanish and, as I read the signs, ol' Thad wants to keep the lid on this particular pot of beans, but that don't mean it's not without danger," he pointed out.

"Don't worry about me, I can take care of myself," she said stoutly, and Wes grinned.

"I can believe that. It'll also make it a mite more of a chore for him to keep tabs on us."

"Speaking of which." Ben came to his feet and moved across to the window, keeping to one side as he peered out to look back the way they had come. "What do you think our shadow is doing now?"

"Shadow?" Mandy asked.

"Fella that followed us from town an' made a real bad job of it."

"You let someone follow you?" She looked bewildered.

"Only when we allow it," Wes replied mildly. "Right now I reckon that ranny is riding hell for leather to tell Tolver where we're at."

"I don't understand," she wailed miserably.

"It's quite simple, ma'am," Ben said

from the window. "It would tip our hand if'n we took out the tail that Tolver had put on us, mebbe prod him into something hasty before we were ready. Better to let him think he's still got the drop on us."

"Ben's right," Wes agreed, climbing to his feet. "A man feels safe when he thinks he's holding all the aces an' that's how we want Tolver to feel. Reckon we'll head back to town now and pick up our things. We'll be back afore dark."

* * *

Sheriff Lyle Rance was standing in the shade of the wooden overhang outside his office when he spied the two return. Chewing on the butt of a dead cigar he retreated into his office and continued watching from the dusty window. Surprise furrowed his brow as he saw them rein in outside Doc Holby's and vanish inside. He ran black-nailed fingers tenderly over a lump on the side of his head. If one of them was hurt he hoped it was the big one. He had a score to settle with that ranny.

After ten minutes or so the two reappeared and continued their journey to the hotel. He waited for them to enter, then flinging the cigar butt down to join others on the littered floor, he left the office.

Doc Holby, MD, looked up with obvious disapproval on his thin, silver-topped face as the door to the surgery burst open and Lyle Rance, belly dancing over the buckle of his belt, entered.

"What did them two varmints want?" He followed the words with a ferocious glare.

In his early sixties, lean and bony beneath a crumpled, black suit, Doc Holby had ministered to the medical needs of Dry Ridge for nigh on thirty years. He had grown up with the town, birthed its children and mopped up its cuts and bruises. He was as much part of the town as was the saloon or general store and as such did not shake before the likes of the bullying Rance.

He fixed Rance with cool dark eyes from beneath silver brows.

"I'd appreciate that you knock afore you come charging in here, Sheriff," he said icily.

"Hardiman and Travis. What did they want?" Rance demanded belligerently, advancing to the front of the desk.

"When a man becomes a doctor he swears a Hippocratic oath that means he don't go shooting his mouth off about his patients or what ails them to other folks. It's called patient confidentiality." Doc Holby sat back in his old chair, rested elbows on its shiny arms and steepled thin fingers before his lips, eyeing Rance.

Lyle Rance smiled thinly.

"Mebbe some smart boy could write that on your tombstone, Doc."

"Don't threaten me, Rance, it won't work," Doc Holby said mildly. "Remember, I'm the only doctor in a hundred miles and you might need me one day."

Rance smirked and leaned, stiff-armed, on the front of the desk.

"Just you remember, Doc, you're getting old; mebbe it's time to get a new doc."

"Are you threatening me, Rance?" The doctor laid his hands flat on the desk top.

"Just giving a little advice on how to live longer," Rance returned. "The law's got a tolerable interest in those boys."

"You mean Thad Tolver has," Doc Holby snapped back.

Rance straightened and eyed the doctor.

"Are you refusing to help a duly appointed officer of the law in the pursuance of his dooty, Doc?" He ran the phrase he had been taught to say by Thad Tolver smoothly off his tongue and with obvious relish. It was one he liked to say and it earned him a wide-eyed look from the medic.

"Good God!" Doc Holby breathed.

"How's that?" Rance cried.

"I was saying, God forbid that I should stand in the way of a duly appointed officer of the law in the pursuance of his duty." He gave up his goading of Rance feeling he had done enough to express his disapproval of Rance's manner. "Purely in the interests of law and order, the big fella got himself a nasty cut on some thorns and came to me to get it looked at and cleaned up." Rance stared at the doctor suspiciously. Doc Holby noted the look and glared. "No need to look like that, Rance. It's what more folks should do. I've seen more limbs lost because folks didn't take the time to tend a cut." He calmly rattled out his rehearsed piece.

"Should'a said so earlier," Rance grumbled darkly.

"So, what's this fella done?" Doc Holby asked.

It was Rance's turn to be obstructive now, but he was less subtle about it.

"None of your damn business," he

grumbled, and strolled out of the surgery feeling pleased with himself.

It was late in the afternoon that the hotel clerk rushed into Rance's office. Rance, three fingers of good whiskey under his belt with another three set to shake hands with them, eyed the clerk belligerently.

"What the hell's caught your britches on fire, Earl?"

"It's them two fellas, Travis and Hardiman, they're gone, Sheriff. Cleaned out their things an' said they wouldn't be needing the rooms agin." Earl ran a hand over his balding forehead. "Watched 'em go, headed south outa town." He paused and waited expectantly for Rance's reaction.

The sheriffs first reaction was alarm, then it struck him that he was only to keep an eye on them in town. If they were gone then so much the better for him.

He smiled at Earl.

"Ain't that a pure shame," he murmured.

"Someone ought to tell Mr Tolver," Earl said anxiously.

"He'll git told. Now why don't you git back to your hotel an' let me get on with sheriffing."

* * *

"I'm afraid your ma and pa didn't die easy. The doctor over at Dry Ridge said they were subjected to excessive brutality," Wes said softly, hating the sound of the truth, seeing her flinch and whiten at his words, but he felt it important she should know the kind of men they were up against. His words were the result of his and Ben's earlier visit to Doc Holby. For Wes it was important to know the exact means of death; it could give an insight into why, and this time it did.

Outside the shadows were lengthening. The setting sun bathed the flanks of the mountains red beneath a dark purple sky. Sunlight slanting across the front of the farmhouse sent angled bars of scarlet through the window to fill the parlour with a red gloom.

Seated on the sofa, Mandy twisted her hands in her lap, tears sparkling in her eyes as she stared up into Wes's set face.

"You mean they were tortured?"

"Sorry, ma'am, but it looks that way," Wes agreed.

"Why would they do that? What harm had my folks done to them?"

"Reckon the killers wanted to make sure that Ray Mallinson didn't give your folks more than just the pendant, like where he found it."

She rose and busied herself with the lamp while Ben drew the curtains on the night. Light filled the room, a cheerful, golden glow that swept the shadows into the corners and danced over the hand-built furniture and scatter of colourful, Indian rugs.

"Is Thad Tolver behind all this, Wes?" she asked, facing him, and Wes shrugged.

"Stacks that way, ma'am, but I don't

accuse a man until I have hard evidence of such. He's a hard man an' totes a mean crew, but that don't make him a killer, yet."

"I understand," she said bitterly, and Wes laid a hand on her shoulder.

"We'll find it," he said, and turned eyes on the silent Ben. "First things first. We've got some coyotes to catch, big fella."

"I'm all for that, shorty," Ben returned with a cheerful grin, their humour bringing a pale smile to her face.

"Don't worry none. Whatever happens we'll be around."

"Take care," she called as they headed for the door and a few minutes later she was on her own.

6

IT began as it always began.

The rock hit the roof with a crash and clattered down the timbered incline before it came to rest on the porch roof. Though she was expecting it the sound made her jump, set her heart a-hammering and mouth dry. She knew what was coming next and cringed.

"Hey, girlie, wanna come out an' play?"

"Naw, she wants us to go in an' join her."

"We'll make a real woman of you, girl."

"Tha's a pure fact."

Laughter, coarse and ragged, followed the words that echoed out of the darkness surrounding the farmhouse from four separate voices. She clenched her fists and compressed her lips in an effort to stop herself from screaming. Even though she knew that tonight was different and that Wes and Ben were out there somewhere, she could not stop the build-up of panic and fear that made her body shake.

The first time it had happened she had rushed to the door with the shot-gun, but the darkness had hidden the callers, only their voices remaining to taunt and goad her. It had made her angry but, as the nights became weeks, the anger turned to fear.

She had laughed in Thad Tolver's face when he had made his offer to buy her out, but with each passing night and the voices grinding at her nerves, her resolve weakened. It was only her own stubbornness and memories of the hard work her parents had put into this place that kept her here, but even that would not be enough without help. Help she now had in the forms of Wes and Ben and the knowledge bolstered her flagging resolve.

Fists hammered at the door and

she leapt to her feet.

"Go away!" she screamed.

The hammering stopped and the hateful laughter filtered in from outside. Where were the two? Why were they taking so long?

* * *

From their place of concealment behind an exposed, weathered rock pile, south-east of the farmhouse, the two had seen the arrival of four shadowy figures. After settling their horses in a grassy hollow the four had crept forward to a position before the farmhouse. They passed a bottle amongst themselves and, after a low, muttered conversation, split up to surround the house. The two waited until the four began their campaign of terror before slipping silently from concealment to deliver a few surprises to the unsuspecting gang.

Ben made the first contact in the narrow passage between the barn and the house. He flattened himself against the end wall of the barn, pressing back into the darkness as the man moved silently down the side of the house. Billy Hapgood was so intent on his own task that the faint whistling of a descending gun barrel did not register until the hard metal crashed against the back of his head. Unfortunately for Billy it was too late by then. Apart from a brief grunt there was no noise. Ben caught Billy as he sagged and lowered him to the ground.

Roy Hapgood, Billy's older, by one year, brother, was smiling hugely as he watched Clem Carson hammer on the front door. The smile was still on his face as the same fate that had befallen his brother happened to him and he toppled from a crouch into an unconscious, sprawled position.

"Ain't no good hidin' in there, girl," Clem called, and darted back to where Roy still crouched. "Dammit, Roy, I say we go in there an' teach her a real lesson," he growled.

"I don't reckon I can allow that," Wes said, lifting his head and grinning at Clem.

Clem gave a startled yell and jumped to his feet, clawing at his gun only to have his wrist caught in an iron grip. Wes used his free hand to good effect, driving it into Clem's flat stomach with zeal. As the breath whistled in an agonized gasp from Clem's lips and he jack-knifed, Wes brought his right knee up into the man's descending face.

The luckless Clem flew backwards and hit the ground with the back of his head and shoulders. The stars in the sky seem to merge in a single bright light. He was vaguely aware of a dark form bending over him; a hand gripped the front of his jacket, hauled him clear of the ground, then a fist slammed into his chin and the night went very dark and silent.

Around the rear of the farmhouse, Tate Grissom hurled another rock on the roof as a figure came around the side and ran at a crouch towards him.

"Reckon that little ol' girl's 'bout ready to get the hell outa here soon, Billy," he chortled.

"I wouldn't count on it," came the grim reply in a strange voice.

Tate turned and his eyes bulged at the giant of a figure that loomed over him.

"You're not Billy," he rattled out in a strangled gasp.

"Mighty observant of you," Ben applauded. The next second a punch that felt like a mule kick lifted Tate off his feet and deposited him, on his back, some yards from where he had been standing. The man made no move to rise. Ben looked down dispassionately at the sprawled man until a boot stirred stones in a stealthy rattle to indicate someone moving down the side of the farmhouse towards him.

Ben darted forward and, with gun in hand, flattened himself against the back wall. A vague form appeared cautiously around the edge of the building and Ben relaxed.

"I take it you've dealt with yours?" he called, sliding the Adams back into its holster as Wes came forward.

"Sleeping like babies," Wes replied with a grin. "Reckon we'll tie 'em up in the barn overnight and maybe stir up a little interest tomorrow."

"How's that?"

"We'll take 'em back to Tolver."

"That sounds more like stirring up a hornets' nest," Ben replied, after a second's startled pause.

"Don't it just," Wes said happily.

* * *

The following morning, Thad Tolver had just sat down to breakfast when a hand came scooting into the room.

"Boss, you gotta come quick," he gasped out breathlessly, dragging his hat from his head, raising a cloud of dust over a platter of potatoes and crispy bacon slices.

Anger flared in Tolver's eyes.

"You'd better have a damn good

reason for busting in here, boy," Tolver snarled at the long-faced hand.

"Come an' see, boss. You gotta come," the man pleaded.

Tolver sighed, eyed a layer of grey dust that had settled over the surface of his coffee and came to his feet.

"This had better be worth it," he growled, but the hand was already on the way out of the room.

As Thad Tolver stepped out into the morning sun all thoughts of his interrupted breakfast were swept from his mind by the sight that greeted him. Ben Travis and Wes Hardiman riding in slowly trailing four sullen-looking men who had been tied in the saddle. Tolver experienced a few seconds of slack-jawed surprise before pulling himself together and pacing forward a few steps as the group came to a halt. News of the arrivals had spread quickly through the bunkhouse and hands tumbled out silently to watch.

"What's the meaning of this?" Tolver

found his voice and glared uneasily at Wes and Ben.

"Might ask you the very same question, Mr Tolver," Wes countered in a bright, easy tone. "Found these here boys skulking about the Fuller place last night being real unfriendly towards Miss Fuller."

"We ain't said nothin', boss," Billy Hapgood spoke up, one eye ringed with black.

Thad Tolver thought quickly.

"Sure, that's right," he agreed, causing the heads of his captured crew to snap up in surprise.

"It is?" Ben said in bewilderment, tossing a quick glance in Wes's direction as Ace Reynolds appeared and settled silently at Tolver's side.

"Had some trouble of late with a bunch of murdering outlaws that've set up camp somewhere in the mountains, the Slater boys. It's reckoned that they were the rannies who murdered Jesse and Meg a while back." He nodded. Haltingly at first and then with growing confidence as he warmed to his theme, the words tumbled from Thad Tolver's lips. "I put my boys out there to keep an eye on the place an' watch over Miss Fuller until them murderers is caught." The words drew an admiring glance from Wes. The old man could think on his feet.

"Now that's right neighbourly of you, Mr Tolver," Wes said.

"Sure is," Ben agreed. "Only it didn't sound too neighbourly to me. Sounded real mean an frightening." He fixed Tolver with flat grey eyes and let Wes take over.

"From the hoorahing going on, reckon I'd agree with Ben, here," Wes added.

Tolver shrugged his thickset shoulders.

"Guess the boys must've taken a bottle to keep out the night chill and had a mite too much. Was that the way of it, boys?" Tolver raised his voice.

"That's how it was, boss," Billy spoke up, with obvious relief in his voice. "Guess we got drunk an' made a tad too much noise. We sure are sorry, boss."

"There you have it, gentlemen. Old John Barleycorn has a lot to answer for. Guess they got a mite boisterous." Tolver beamed at Wes and Ben. "I reckon we have a misunderstanding here. The boys were only funning to my way of thinking and went a little too far. They'll lose a week's pay and spend the next month riding line. See if'n that don't straighten 'em out. That sound reasonable to you?" He eyed the two keenly.

"Guess it's the best we can expect," Wes said.

Tolver motioned to a man.

"Williams, get them outa my sight." He watched as the man came forward and slashed away their bonds with a knife and the four rode across the yard towards the cookhouse. "It was mighty lucky you happened to be at the Fullers', otherwise no telling what might have happened," he mused. "How come you were there?" Now it was Tolver's turn to play cat and mouse.

"Like we said earlier, Mr Tolver, we're looking to set up a freight office and the Fuller place is just right for the job. Miss Fuller agreed and we moved out there. Lucky we did as things turned out," Wes explained.

"She sold it to you?" There was a sharpness in Tolver's voice.

"Made an agreement," Wes corrected. "We'll be staying there while we look about. Makes it suitable all around, don't you agree?"

"If you say so," Tolver said tightly, clearly not happy with the turn of events, but unable to raise any objections.

"Good, then we'll be neighbours, Mr Tolver. Well, now we've sorted out all our misunderstandings, Ben an' I'll be moseying along. Got some looking around to do afore nightfall." Wes touched the brim of his hat. "Guess we'll be seeing each other again, Mr Tolver." With that parting shot Wes knee'd his mount forward and with

Ben following the two rode away from the ranch.

Thad Tolver, the morning sun silvering his white hair, watched the two ride away, brown eyes bleak and expressionless. By the time the two had dwindled to specks against the grandeur of the lofty peaks, the watching hands had disappeared to talk amongst themselves about the incident. Only Ace Reynolds, the gunman, remained with Tolver. Finally Tolver turned his gaze on the silent gunman.

"I'm thinking that something will have to be done 'bout those two jaspers."

A cold smile spread across Reynolds' pale face.

"Anything you say, Mr Tolver," Reynolds whispered.

"No, no, my friend. We only use your special skills as a last resort." Tolver smiled in the direction the two had taken, a vicious light sparking in his eyes. "I think it's 'bout time they were introduced properly to Mr Mahonney and his friends. Send Billy to the camp and get Mahonney to organize a little welcoming party for them." The smile soured on his face as he looked once again at Reynolds. "It would appear that our sheriff has fallen down on the job again. I should've been told 'bout them leaving town. You and I, Mr Reynolds, are going to see what Rance has to say for himself."

* * *

There were two trails. Two hours' riding had brought the pair to a high-walled pass above the tree-line of the mountain range. Once through the pass they found themselves entering a huge canyon that split the range from east to west. It was here the single trail branched, one way snaking down into the canyon, the other leading up to the northern canyon rim.

"Which way?" Ben asked, turning to Wes.

"Reckon we take one each an' meet back here afore sundown."

Ben nodded and elected to take the high trail. They talked for a while and then set off on their separate ways, little knowing what fate had in store for them.

For Wes, the trail down to the canyon bottom was steep and littered with loose scree and rock that caused the horse to slide and stumble. In the end Wes dismounted and led the horse until they reached the flat of the canyon bottom.

The canyon was perhaps a half-mile wide, but the sheer, towering walls made it seem narrower than it was. The illusion was further helped by the build up of rock and blown sand that lined the base of the walls on either side, decorated with patches of tough gamma grass and thorny scrub. Due to the lay of the canyon, the sun shone its full length and the trapped heat sucked the moisture from his body. Wes ignored the discomfort, eyes studying the ground, searching for signs that others had passed this way, but he found nothing.

He continued on letting the paint pick its own pace, content to laze in the saddle and let his eyes do the work. He was not sure what he was looking for, but Tolver was running a gang of miners and trying to pass them off as ranch hands, the stranglehold of fear he had on the town, the use of Lyle Rance to discourage strangers to stay, the deaths of the Fullers. He felt in his bones that it was all to do with Cordoba's Treasure, but how was a problem to chew on.

He mulled it all over in his head and still hadn't come to a definite conclusion when the explosion ripped through the dry, sun-scorched air.

He had allowed himself to become a little drowsy in the saddle, mind ranging over a number of possibilities that he dismissed as soon as they came, so he was not ready for the concussive report that set the paint rearing and neighing in fright and sent him tumbling from the saddle. As he hit the ground on his back, jarring the breath from his body, he saw, high up on the northern rim of the canyon, a blossom of smoke and dust unfurl. Directly overhead it spread outwards against the narrow blue gash of sky.

The paint, free of its burden, took off leaving a winded rider to watch as a huge section of the canyon wall broke free and began to fall trailing a thick, writhing trail of dust in its wake.

As the echoes of the explosion bounced from wall to wall and beat into his dazed brain, tiny stones, shaken loose from lower down, began to rain down about him.

Wes scrambled to his feet looking around desperately knowing that in a few seconds tons of rocks would smash his body to a pulp and there was nothing he could do to avoid it.

7

BEN, astride his big black, urged the powerful animal up the narrow trail that climbed between narrow rocky walls. The trail angled north-westerly away from the canyon. Occasionally it would flatten out allowing man and beast some respite and then continue ever upwards. By the time it came out above the canyon both man and horse were covered in a film of sweat. Ben brought the black to a halt.

A mile or a little less to the south, he could see the rim of the canyon and beyond that a spectacular vista of jagged, broken peaks painted with thick streaks of black where shadows hid from the sun in folds and creases in the rock.

Peak threw shadows on peak as they rolled away like some wild, petrified sea to a distant horizon, gradually losing definition in a purplish haze the further away they got.

Ben drank in the savage splendour of the view. Some of the more distant peaks were tipped with white glistening snow that made them stand out starkly against the fierce blue of the sky. He sucked cool air from a soft breeze into his hot lungs letting its soft caress cool the heat of his body; a luxury denied Wes in the sweltering, canyon bottom.

Ben knee'd the black forward across the flat ridge, angling away from the canyon rim to where he could see the tips of tall, piñon pines poking up their dark green heads. After a while the ground began to buckle and ridge as though it had been formed in a boiling pot and allowed to cool. Rocky walls closed about him as he began a gentle descent towards the pines.

"Now isn't that a foine sight for a lonely man? A visitor is it? Welcome,

Mr Travis, we've been waiting for you."

Ben hauled the black to a halt in surprise as the smiling figure of Red Mahonney appeared on the narrow trail ahead. Two others, Winchesters held in readiness, flanked him. Their faces were not smiling.

"G'day, Red," Ben greeted. "What are you doing here?"

"'Tis a question I should be asking you," Red countered.

A noise from behind had Ben turn his head. Four more dour-faced, rifle-toting men blocked any idea of a retreat.

"What's going on, Red? Why the guns?" Ben asked innocently, trying to maintain an air of surprised innocence. "You know we're looking for a trail over the mountains." It puzzled Ben that the Irishman had not asked the whereabouts of Wes. It filled him with foreboding.

"'Tis the end of the trail you have reached." There was mocking sorrow in Red's voice and Ben stiffened in the saddle. He was considering what to do next when the problem was taken out of his hands. From above a rope dropped over his shoulders and he was dragged from the saddle, arms pinned to his sides. His weight carried him against the rock wall with a jarring crash that rattled every bone in his body and then, none too gently, he was dropped to the ground.

Pain and fury blended in his eyes as he twisted up his head to see the grinning face of the rope thrower some twenty feet above him. He scrambled awkwardly to his feet and faced Red. The distant crump of an explosion reached his ears and made the ground tremble for an instant beneath his feet.

"What the hell was that?" he demanded of the smiling Red.

"Ah, well that would be Mr Hardiman reaching the end of his trail." Laughter from the other men accompanied the words.

Chest heaving, Ben glared at the

Irishman and then lunged forward against the pull of the rope.

Taken by surprise, the rope thrower above felt himself jerked forward and with a wailing cry of fear was torn from his perch into space. He sailed over Ben's head and hit the rocky ground headfirst. There was an ominous cracking sound as the man's neck broke. Struggling to free himself from the rope, his efforts were rewarded with a rifle butt to the back of his head and, with a grunt of pain, Ben toppled, unconscious, to the ground.

* * *

As the mass of rock broke free of the canyon wall and plummeted towards him, a desperate plan formed in Wes's mind. The base of the canyon wall at this point sloped gently inwards. At the top of the rock and scree slope that lined it there was a narrow, horizontal gouge in the rock. He began scrambling up the slope before the plan had time to jell in his mind and, as the first sections of rock began to crash about him, he threw himself down and rolled into the niche, covering his head with his arms. He wondered grimly if he was laying himself out in his own tomb, but it was too late to worry about that now.

Pressed into the depression as far as he could go the mass of rock arrived. It hit the ground with a thunderous roar that punched shock waves through his body. The awesome sound pierced the protective covering of hand over ears and beat into his brain. As a thick, choking darkness engulfed him and bouncing rocks slammed into his unprotected back, panic ripped through him. He was going to die!

* * *

Water poured from a canteen splashed over Ben's face and brought him back to groggy consciousness. He was hauled to his feet, relieved of his gunbelt and, with hands bound tightly behind his back, set astride his horse. To discourage any attempt to escape, a rope was fastened about his neck and the other end tied to the saddlehorn of an accompanying rider. Thus he was led away swaying dazedly in the saddle, hammers beating in his skull from the effect of the earlier blow.

By the time they had passed down through the trees and emerged into a flat valley the hammers had ceased and only a dull, bearable ache remained and even that was momentarily forgotten at the sight that met his eyes.

Ringed by high peaks, the peak directly across as they emerged from the trees was of fresh, virgin rock, its original weathered face blasted into with dynamite until it formed a huge, blind cave a hundred feet high and as much wide. Massive piles of rocks formed a wide semicircular wall before the monstrous cave. Ben only caught a glimpse of the area in front the cave before they descended lower and the walls of rubble, fully thirty feet high, hid it. The glimpse had been enough for him to see men working within the mighty mouth of the cave.

As they followed the curve of the rock-debris wall, Ben noted men with rifles spaced along it, looking inwards. He could only wonder at what was going on here. It made no sense.

A group of buildings appeared ahead. A long, wooden bunkhouse, facing a cookhouse, with a small cabin and windowless storeshed at the far end. In the shape of a U, they were approaching the open end of it. Behind lay a barn and corral where a number of horses cropped on a patch of grass. Men appeared from the bunkhouse as the group rode past, curious eyes on Ben.

"Home, sweet home," Red sang out, as they came to a halt at a hitch rail set before the cabin.

Ben swung down awkwardly from his horse and, as it was led away, the noose was removed from his throat. A figure emerged from the cabin and Ben's heart skipped a beat as Thad Tolver, cigar in mouth, moved towards him, a smile on his face. Not far behind came the pale-faced gunman, Ace Reynolds, who moved into position beside the rancher as he came to a halt.

"How nice of you to drop in, Mr Travis," he said around the cigar.

Ben forced a smile.

"It was kinda hard to ignore the invitation."

"Pity Mr Hardiman couldn't come, but I understand he had some rather weighty business to attend to." He laid emphasis on the word weighty, enjoying his own joke. "Dangerous places, mountains. They sometimes fall on the unexpected and Mr Hardiman, alas, did not expect it. Is that not correct, Mr Mahonney?"

"Indeed it is, sor. T'was a terrible shame, a nasty accident. All that rock falling on him." He shook his head and managed a doleful expression. "'Tis more than a headache he'll be having now." Red chuckled at his own joke.

Ben felt a lead weight settle on his stomach.

"You won't get away with this," he said hotly.

"Get away with what, Mr Travis?" Tolver asked blandly, removing the cigar from his lips. "What are we getting away with?"

"You tell me," Ben countered.

Tolver regarded him in silence for a few moments.

"Looking for a freight trail across the mountains? Bullshit, Mr Travis," he murmured.

"If'n you say so," Ben replied tightly.

"Oh I do, indeed I do. Why would someone interested in opening a freight line show even more interest in the deaths of the Fullers? The good doctor and I had a very informative talk earlier today. He was very co-operative, eventually."

Ben felt a coldness wash over him.

"What do you mean?"

"I'm sure his funeral will be well attended, but it was bound to happen.

He was getting old, horse was probably spooked by a rattler; he fell off and broke his neck. Tragic accident." He chuckled.

Ben felt his mouth gape at the man's cold-blooded confession to murder; second murder if he accepted what they had said about Wes.

"You're mad," Ben gasped out.

"Just protecting what is mine," Tolver replied, "and Cordoba's Treasure is mine, Mr Travis." Tolver laughed as Ben reacted to the words, unable to stop a start of surprise. "I expect the pendant that Mallinson found and got away with brought you and the late Mr Hardiman on the scene. No matter denying it as the reason is of little consequence. Come, I'll satisfy your curiosity; after all you may be the one who eventually finds it. Bring him." The last words were uttered to a pair of guards behind Ben. Rifle barrels prodded his back and ushered him in the wake of Tolver who was hurrying towards the rock barrier. Crude steps had been made in the side and Ben followed the rancher up to a flat platform at the top. From here they overlooked the vast cave and the men working within its depths. The sight of them brought a grim look to Ben's face. Even from this distance he could see they were forced to work bare-footed with chains about their ankles watched by guards toting rifles and bullwhips.

He tore his gaze from the pitiful labour force and noticed for the first time that the rear wall of the cave was peppered with a series of holes that, before its destruction, must have represented a vast tunnel system.

"I will assume you know the legend of Cordoba Mr Travis, and his subsequent flight across these mountains with the stolen treasure. He was never seen or heard of again. Something happened and he, his men, and the treasure vanished.

"I spent a lot of time and money in establishing the route he took and it led me to this place. It was a tremendous cave and tunnel system.

I began searching the tunnels only to realize it could take a lifetime to search them all. I looked around for a quicker way and this is it. The easiest way would be to take the mountain apart." Tolver nodded to himself. "So I hired Mr Mahonney and his boys and did just that."

"You are mad," Ben said flatly, repeating an earlier statement.

"Perhaps, Mr Travis," Tolver conceded. "A man has to be mad to come to this godforsaken land in the first place; face Indians, outlaws and the goddam weather to build a ranch and raise cattle."

"That ain't no call to murder folks," Ben snapped back bluntly, and Tolver laughed.

"A few no-accounts. Out here only the strongest survive and I aim to be the strongest. I take what I want an' that includes Cordoba's Treasure."

"If'n you can find it," Ben cut back, and Tolver rounded on him angrily.

"I'll find it all right, Travis," he

snarled. "Each day we bring down a little more of the mountain and one day the treasure will be among the rubble. Cordoba may have been clever hiding the treasure in all those tunnels, but it ain't gonna be hidden for long." Tolver's anger lightened. "Who knows, Mr Freight Man, you may be the one to find it."

"Seems like one fella did," Ben goaded, and Tolver's face darkened again.

"I like spirit in a man, Mr Travis," he hissed. "I wonder how long it will last in you?"

"You won't get away with this, Tolver."

"You have a habit of repeating yourself, Mr Travis," he sighed. "But, as I pointed out earlier, I already have. Now all that remain are just a few loose ends to tidy up. A telegram to the people who sent you, in a week or so, telling how you and Mr Hardiman went into the mountains and never returned and how an exhaustive search failed to find you. But first of all the Fuller girl must be taken care of. Time for the outlaws who have been terrorizing the country to pay her a visit. We'll give her a good funeral along with the doctor."

"She has nothing to do with this," Ben cried heatedly.

"Just making sure. Loose ends, Mr Travis, loose ends. Take him away, Mr Mahonney and put him to work."

Rage flared in Ben's eyes. Even with his hands tied he was prepared to lunge at the rancher until the barrel of a rifle was thrust under his chin.

"You'd better make sure that when this is over that I'm good and dead, Tolver, because I'll be coming after you."

"Don't worry, Mr Travis, you will be." Tolver turned away and Red Mahonney stepped in front of Ben.

"Come on, me boyo, there's an old friend waiting to greet you, to be sure." He swung Ben around until he faced the steps he had climbed up and there at the bottom, a grin on his fat face, stood the huge Ox. "'Tis the pleasure of your company the Ox has been waiting for. Let's not keep him waiting."

8

WES sat hunched in a foetal position, knees drawn up to his chin in a tiny, cramped space. That he was still alive was cause for elation, but that feeling soon gave way to a hopelessness as the confines of the space closed in around him.

Sweat trickled down his face and soaked into his clothing in the stuffy, airless surround. The warm darkness enveloped him like the thick, choking folds of a shroud. He felt around and found that a slab of rock had fallen at an angle against the cliff face forming a sloping wall before where he lay, protecting him from the main fall of rock. He was bruised and battered, sore in a dozen places, but otherwise unharmed. In his present position he was not sure if that was a blessing or a curse.

In the pressing, cloying darkness he rubbed sweat from his eyes with a dusty, trembling hand. The only crumb of dark comfort lay in the weapon holstered at his side. If the worst came to the worst, at least he had a way to end it all. He thrust the thought from his mind, took a deep breath and extended his arms out sideways; he felt the knobbly surface of rock in both directions before his arms were fully extended.

To the right a rock moved slightly at his touch. He tested it gently, rocking it back and forth like a wobbly tooth until finally it came loose and fell with a crash to the ground. Dust and rock fragments slithered after it making a stealthy, hissing rattle.

He pulled another rock free and extended his arm into the hole. Sweat ran into his eyes and trickled saltily over his dry lips. Ignoring it he continued clawing and scraping at the rock wall working more fragments free. Dust filled the air around him, stinging his eyes and scraping like tiny claws at the back of his dry, parched throat. It was getting difficult to breathe now and woolly lightness filled his brain. He was beginning to suffocate.

The terrible realization made him work faster. In desperation, his arm now fully extended into the hole, he pulled and pushed at the rock, and it was on a push that a rock fell away and a shaft of light appeared. He pulled in his arm and squirmed into a kneeling position, left shoulder pushed hard against the angled slab, as he placed his face to the hole and sucked fresh air into his burning lungs.

The hole on the inside was about a foot across, but considerably less on the outside. Forcing himself to work at a slower pace he carefully enlarged the inner opening, placing the rocks behind him.

A fierce surge of elation set the adrenalin flowing within him; maybe all was not lost. Carefully he eased the rocks away from the base of the widening tunnel as he moved towards the opening. With head and shoulders and one arm in he began to enlarge the outer opening. More light flooded in, illuminating his face sheened with sweat that, combined with the dust, fell in muddy drips from his chin.

As he worked he became even more conscious that, at any minute, the rock build-up above could collapse on to him and crush the life from his body. The thought turned the muddy sweat to rolling beads of ice. He put the thought from his mind and concentrated on the task. Finally, judging the tunnel in the rockfall wide enough, he withdrew into his tiny cave and settled his beating heart with a few deep breaths. It was now or never. Thrusting both arms into the tunnel he began to wriggle forward. Sharp edges snagged his clothing and, at one point from above, came an ominous, creaking grind as shifting rocks rubbed together.

His hands were out, then elbows, then head and shoulders and he could see that he was three-quarters of the way up a huge slope of rock that ran to form a wall across the floor of the canyon. With the bulky, upper part of his body free, he heard the rumbling grind and a weight settled on his lower legs still in the tunnel.

Panic seized him. A rock tumbled down from above just missing his head. The upper part of the rockfall was beginning to cave in. Throwing caution to the winds he began hauling himself out kicking as much as he could with his trapped legs. He felt his legs come free and, literally, threw himself down the rock slope as, seconds later, the upper part of the rockfall shifted and the tunnel collapsed, spitting dust and tossing rock fragments in his wake.

He hardly felt the pain as he tumbled down the slope. It was only at the bottom as he clambered stiffly to his feet that his body protested from a hundred different places, but a huge smile was on his face. He had made it and was still alive. The smile distilled into an ugly snarl of rage and anger. Someone had tried to kill him and it was just unfortunate for them that they had failed for they would not get a second chance. He wondered about Ben. Had the big man suffered a like attack and survived?

He brushed dust from his clothes, wincing as he touched bruises. He was glad to see his paint cropping at a sparse patch of yellowing grass a hundred yards down the canyon. Wes gave a whistle; the animal lifted its head in his direction, ears pricked and, with a welcoming snort, cantered to greet Wes as he stumbled on to flat ground. He rubbed the animal's velvety muzzle before unslinging his canteen and gulping thirstily at the squat neck. He upturned his face and poured water over it feeling it roll down his back and soak the collar of his shirt. It felt great. Afterwards he pulled an old blue bandanna from a pocket, ran it over his face and swung astride the paint.

His main concern now was to find Ben. He was not sure how long he had been buried; one hour, maybe two but, by the time he returned to the dividing of the trails where they were supposed to meet, the sky was reddening in the west. It would soon be nightfall.

He waited restlessly until the sky to the east began to darken and purple shadows began to ooze from the rocks and spill across the ground. No sign of Ben and it would be suicide to try and ride the high trail in the dark looking for him. Reluctantly he turned the paint and headed west on the trail that would take him out of the mountains and on to the plains. He would return at first light.

* * *

As Wes struggled to free himself from the rockfall, Ben found himself standing before the huge, bloated figure of Ox. The big, oafish individual held a stout hickory cudgel in one hand tapping its thick, knobbly head into the palm of the other.

"Sure am glad to meet you agin, mister," Ox wheezed, in his rasping, throaty voice.

"I'm just plumb glad I could make it," Ben returned with an amiable grin. "Sure sorry we can't shake hands."

Ox frowned. The smiling face upset him. He lashed out with the cudgel, ramming it into Ben's stomach. Ben saw the move coming and was able to steel his muscles, but even so the blow hurt and doubled him over. Ox was gratified to see the smile become a grimace.

"Don' mention it," Ox replied. "We'll get better acquainted real soon." He laughed at his own joke in a series of wheezy chuckles.

"I can't wait," Ben gasped.

Ben was taken to the huge, shallow cave that dynamite had carved into the side of the peak. Close to it was awesome, but he had little time to stand and stare. His boots and socks were removed and manacles fastened to his ankles with a length of clanking chain between that allowed him to shuffle. Only then were his wrists cut loose.

"'Tis a simple enough task that we'll have you doing." Red Mahonney approached him. "You clear the rock that is blasted from the rock face and pile it along the base of the outer wall." Red indicated to where thin, shirtless men were loading rocks into a wooden wheelbarrow. "I'm sure you'll be getting the hang of it soon enough and if you find any gold trinkets you sing out."

"What song would you like?" Ben said, and was rewarded by a crippling blow from Ox's hickory club. He swung around on the man, eyes dark with anger, fists balled at his sides.

"We're gonna meet when I ain't got these things on my legs, fat man," he snarled.

"I hope so," Ox returned in his whispering tone.

"Boys, boys, let's not be arguing, there's work to be done." Red stepped between them. "Get him to work." He said this to a pair of gun-toting guards who moved forward and prodded Ben towards the cliff face.

Other workers paid him scant attention.

"Ben, Ben Travis, over here."

Ben snapped up his head and focused eyes on a bare-chested, shaggy-bearded individual dumping rock into a barrow.

"Pete, is that you?" Ben clanked his way across gingerly, sharp fragments cutting into the soles of his feet.

Pete Mullins gave a tiny nod of his head, eyes darting about.

"It's me, but don't let on we know each other."

Ben looked around. The two guards had retreated and Red and Ox had already reached the wall of rock.

"Good to see you, Pete," Ben acknowledged, as he set to work loading the barrow.

"I guess Ray made it then."

"Sort of," Ben replied, and quickly told the story of how Ray Mallinson had arrived, half dead, at the Fuller farm.

"What about Wes?"

"They buried him under an avalanche," Ben replied grimly.

Pete was about to say something else when he caught sight of a guard eyeing them suspiciously.

"No more talk. We're being watched," Pete mouthed, grabbed the handles of the barrow and wheeled it away.

The remainder of the daylight hours were spent in the same, mindless drudgery of rock clearing and Ben learned that as soon as the area was cleared another section of the rock face would be blasted in the search for the elusive treasure and the whole process would start again.

By nightfall Ben felt as though he was walking on fire. The soles of his feet were cut and lacerated so that every step was agony and his ankles had been rubbed raw by the leg irons. Supper turned out to be a weak, watery soup served up with chunks of stale, rock-hard bread that needed to be soaked in the soup before it could be eaten. Tasteless as it was, Ben ate it up. Afterwards he removed coat and shirt and proceeded to tear the shirt into strips that he bound about his sore feet.

"You get used to it in the end." Pete came across, chains clanking on the ground and threw himself next to Ben. He was followed by a younger man, ribs showing starkly through the flesh of his narrow chest. "Glen Meachen, the senator's son," Pete introduced.

The group rested where they worked, huddled against the rock face. There were some ten men in all, thin, dispirited creatures. A semicircle of kerosene lamps formed a barrier of yellow light within which they rested. The light filled eye-sockets with dark pools of shadow making faces seem more gaunt than they were.

"If'n you've come to help us, Mr

Travis, you're sure going 'bout it a strange way," Glen said.

"Reckon you're right there," Ben agreed bitterly. He stared around. Beyond the glare of the lamps the darkness seemed even thicker, hiding the guards who Ben knew would be there, waiting and watching. He looked across at Pete. "How did Ray manage to get away?"

"Straight up the rock face," Pete replied with a smile. "We uncovered a vertical fault in the rock. A deep crack wide enough to fit a man into. Ray reckoned to make it out of here by way of the crack. He reckoned that if'n he could get above the limit of the lamplight he could get away an' get help." The smile dropped from Pete's face. "He surely did it, but it cost him. The fault's gone now, blasted away, not that they knew how he done it, figured he'd slipped past the guards in the night. It was after that that they fitted us with leg irons so's it couldn't happen again."

"Sure is a shame that after all that the help that came wasn't so good," Ben muttered, clenching his fists in frustration.

"No good blaming yourself; Tolver's got a pretty good setup going here," Pete pointed out.

"How come Ray had a piece of Cordoba's Treasure with him?"

"Tolver reckons it was a stray item an' the rest is still up there somewhere waiting to be found."

"Seems likely," Ben agreed with a nod.

"Seems that way," Pete said, "only it ain't."

Ben studied the bearded face with a frown.

"Ain't what?"

"What it seems." Pete gave a secretive smile and sank his voice. "We found Cordoba's Treasure a long time ago."

* * *

In the quietness of the night-shrouded farmhouse, Mandy Fuller listened to the soft, almost furtive creak of timbers settling and wondered where the pair had got to. She had expected them home a long time ago and now the waiting had begun to grind on her nerves. More than once she had wandered out into the cool darkness to stand and listen only to return inside when the cold shivered her flesh.

A log fire crackled and spat in the grate. She stood and stared into the red, glowing embers.

The only other source of light in the room was that thrown out by a single lamp on the table top. Its soft, mellow glow left corners and rafters wrapped in gloom.

The quietness was such that when the window shattered it was like a bomb going off.

She whirled, heart thudding in her breast, unable to suppress a shriek of alarm. Flames leapt up the curtains in a flare that hurt her eyes; someone had thrown a lighted brand through the window, catching the curtains alight before it came to rest on the wooden boarding of the floor.

For a few seconds she stood rooted to the spot staring with fascination as the flames licked about the tinder-dry rafters. She heard hurried footsteps on the porch outside, caught the pungent whiff of kerosene then, with a dull crump, flames leapt up outside the window.

Smoke began to fill the room and sting her eyes. Clapping a hand to her mouth she ran for the door, dragging it open only to stagger back into the room as a wall of flame barred her way. Coughing and spluttering she made a dash for the back of the house as, overhead, flames ran along the rafters.

Smoke whirled after her and she reached the back door and clawed it open throwing herself out into a world of flickering, orange shadows. She stumbled and fell to the ground, coughing and choking. Rough hands hauled her up and held her from behind. Figures blurred by the tears that filled her eyes moved before her.

"Now ain't that a pure shame," a sardonic voice cooed. "Lucky we wus passin' by. Bring her an' let's get the hell outa here."

As she was forced to move she didn't need to be able to see who the owner of the voice was, she recognized it as being one of the callers in the night. Tolver's men had returned and this time they meant business. Clad in working britches and a check shirt, she was bundled into the saddle of a waiting horse, hands lashed and bound to the saddle horn, a dirty bandanna drawn tight about her lips.

Roy Hapgood turned in the saddle, his thick, bristly face red in the leaping flames.

"Ain't no boys gonna come riding by to save you this time, lady," he growled. "You shoulda gone when you had the chance." He grinned evilly at her. "Happen it's better for us this way. Mr Tolver gets your land an' we get you an' that's a pleasure we've been waiting on, ain't that right boys?" There were nods and grins from two of the other three riders; the third, Clem Carson, spoke up.

"Mr Tolver said she was to burn in the farmhouse. He ain't gonna like this."

Roy Hapgood turned on the man.

"Well, what he don't know ain't gonna hurt him. She won't be squawking her mouth off none, so if'n you don't want a piece of this filly then that's fine by me, but you keep your face shut. You're in this as much as we are, so just you remember that."

Clem licked his lips.

"I ain't gonna say nothing, Roy," he said.

"Good, then let's ride. We lay up at the line shack for a few days like Mr Tolver planned and she'll help while away the time." He laughed coarsely and she felt a block of ice settle in her stomach. It would have been better for her had she died in the burning farmhouse.

Tears filled her eyes as the riders moved off into the darkness, the reins of her horse in the hands of Billy Hapgood. Alone and helpless there would be no one to come to her aid now when she most needed someone.

9

"YOU'VE found it already?" Ben could hardly believe what he was hearing. He delivered Pete a hard look. "Then why in tarnation are we taking this mountain to pieces?" His voice rose a little causing concern to leap into Pete's eyes.

"Keep your voice down," he pleaded.

"The answer's simple, Mr Travis," Glen broke in softly. "The moment they get their hands on the treasure, we're dead. They're not gonna let us walk out of here and tell the world what's been going on."

Ben nodded slowly.

"We figured that by hiding it and continuing to work we'd stand a better chance of someone finding us," Pete took up the story. "We were lucky. It's in a chest an' it came down without busting open an' we managed to keep it buried until nightfall an' we could hide it away."

"So where did you hide it? Don't seem much of place to hide things with the guards about." His eyes went to the cave.

Pete smiled and shook his head.

"Not there, it don't go back more'n ten feet. Like I said, we waited until the last shift when it was almost dark and took it on a barrow to the outer wall. Reckoned if'n they started poking about the last place they'd look is right under their feet."

Ben threw the pair an admiring look.

"That's real smart thinking," he applauded.

"We thought so at the time," Pete replied. "It's now buried deep in the wall, but pretty soon now there ain't gonna be any more mountain to blow up an' when that happens Tolver ain't gonna have much use for us, treasure or no treasure. We gave ourselves breathing room, but that's all. A few more days an' then they'll be using us for target practice. We need a miracle now, Ben, if'n we're to get out of this alive."

* * *

Tired and feeling every jolt, Wes let his paint settle to its own pace as they travelled across the dark plain towards the Fuller farmhouse. Once out of the mountains and he could relax, tiredness wrapped weighty folds about his battered body. Beneath a star-splashed canopy of black he dozed in the saddle, skirting the Tolver ranch many miles to the north.

He saw the red glow in the sky to the east and with tiredness forgotten, aches and pains temporarily pushed aside, he kicked heels into the paint's flanks and set the animal galloping through the darkness.

By the time he reached the farmhouse the building was a blazing inferno that sent out a barrier of heat in all directions for a hundred yards. As Wes threw himself from the saddle the roof collapsed with a roar, sending twisting eddies of sparks high into the night. All he could do was stand there in helpless frustration and watch the building burn not knowing if Mandy was in there or not. Bathed in the Hadean glow he prowled the perimeter of the heat barrier like a caged animal.

At one stage he kicked a can that lay in the grass and one sniff told him all he needed to know. The fire had been deliberate. A hardness settled across his features, reflected in the flames that danced in his bleak eyes. Someone was going to pay for this and that someone was Thad Tolver.

By dawn the fire had burned itself out; all that remained of the farmhouse was the blackened stone chimney breast rising forlornly from the smouldering ashes. Wes poked about through the burnt-out ruins searching for the grim evidence of human remains, but found nothing to indicate Mandy had perished in the conflagration. Heartened, he cast about beyond the ashes of the farmhouse and finally found the tracks of five horses heading in a north-westerly direction. They could only belong to whoever had fired the farmhouse. These unknown riders had answers he needed to know, perhaps even to the whereabouts of Mandy Fuller.

Wes mounted up and, as dawn brightened from the east, set out in pursuit of the five.

* * *

The dynamite charges exploded high up on the rock face. Three explosions that buffeted their ears with sound and bounced about the surrounding walls. In the early morning light great blossoms of white unfolded from the rock face, grew and merged into a single white cloud from whose depths dropped a deadly 'rain' of stone. Tons of rock fell to earth raising a choking swirl of fine dust that billowed out to the boulder wall where Ben and the other workers had been herded. Chained together, while the guards sheltered behind the wall, they could do nothing but cower, backs to the swirl and wait for the dust to settle.

Later, covered in a white shroud of dust, tears streaming from dust-reddened eyes, the central chain was removed and they were sent out to begin the back-breaking task of sifting through the rubble and clearing it away.

Pete's face was grim as he stared up at the cliff face.

"I think we've just run out of time," he said bleakly. Ben followed his gaze not quite understanding the other's tone of defeat until Pete continued, "There are no more tunnels up there; no more reason to keep us alive."

The words beat into Ben's brain as he stared up at the rough but unblemished rock face that loomed above; the last series of explosions had erased all traces of the tunnels that had once cut into the mountains.

* * *

Roy Hapgood gulped noisily at the neck of a whiskey bottle, Adam's apple jerking behind the dirty skin of his neck, eyes on the bound form of Mandy.

The old line shack of the north-western limit of Tolver's land lay in the shadows of the towering mountain peaks against a backdrop of oak. The shack was little more than a huge, wooden crate with a door. There were no windows. It was a place to shelter from the elements when the weather turned bad and nothing more. At an angle beside it a second building, longer and open-fronted, divided into a series of stalls, provided shelter for the horses. At present the five horses did not require the doubtful shelter of the low barn; turned out into a corral on the edge of the trees, they contentedly cropped at the grass.

"Hey, gimme some of that, Brother," Billy sang out, running a hand across his whiskery lips and staring at Mandy. He stood leaning against the side wall of the shack while Roy occupied the only table. Clem Carson and Tate Grissom lounged either side of the open door through which the only source of light came, spreading inwards and barely reaching the rear of the shack. Apart from a double bunk bed set against the shadowy rear wall, the table and two chairs, one of which Mandy was lashed in, were all the furnishings the shack contained.

Roy lowered the bottle on to the table top and with a quick movement slid it towards his brother. Billy grabbed it up and with a wolfish grin sucked at the neck. He hardly tasted the harsh spirit as it burned its way to his stomach, his thoughts were on other more basic things. His eyes lingered on the swell of the girl's breasts behind the material of her check shirt. Mandy saw the look in his shadowed face and quailed inwardly. The gag had been taken from her mouth and she sat in stony, wooden-faced silence.

"Hey, don' drink it all," Tate Grissom called, and Billy tossed the bottle across. Grissom caught it deftly and took a couple of hefty swallows. Only Clem Carson remained silent, making no call for the bottle. He had barely said a word since they had arrived, standing tight-lipped and nervous by the door. He had no heart in what they planned for the girl, but he was powerless to do anything to stop it.

Billy ran the back of a hand across his lips and moved purposefully towards the bound girl. She watched his approach with frightened eyes, determined not to give them the satisfaction of seeing or hearing the fear she felt.

"'Bout time you an' I got better acquainted, girl," Billy said, passion making his voice hoarse.

"Show her what she's been missing, Billy," Grissom called out.

"I intend to do that all right," Billy bragged, standing over her and staring down into her defiant, upturned face. "How's 'bout it, girl, ready for a real man?" He grabbed her hair at the back and forced her head back even more, before pushing his face down on to hers, crushing her lips hard against his. Whiskey, sweat and foul breath caught in her nose.

She tried to turn her head away, but his painful grip on her hair prevented all but the smallest movement.

"Give it to her, Brother," Roy sang out, amusement dancing in his dark eyes.

Billy raised his head and, while staring arrogantly around at his brother, ran his free hand over her breasts, digging his fingers into the soft but firm mounds beneath the fabric of her shirt.

"I aim to, Brother," he said breathlessly.

Mandy felt her flesh cringe beneath the man's hard, painful caress. Tears pricked her eyes. Billy's face descended on hers again, but this time she was ready for him. She parted her lips slightly and, in a quick, lightning move, she bit down on his lower lip.

With an almost feminine shriek Billy leapt away from her and cannoned against the side wall, blood spurting between hands cupped at his mouth.

It was a few seconds before the others realized what had happened and Billy confirmed it through cupped hands.

"The bitch bit me," he shouted, eyes watering from the pain. His statement brought a bellow of laughter from Roy, and Tate Grissom was grinning from ear to ear.

Roy eyed the defiantly smiling Mandy.

"Hell, she's got spirit," he sang out, laughing.

"Ain't she though," Tate Grissom cried. "Hell, tha's the best yet."

Billy was not amused. The initial shock and pain over, he removed his hands to reveal a bloody chin from a badly bitten lower lip that was already puffing up. Hate replaced the pain in his eyes as he glared at Mandy.

"Goddam, bitch," he snarled, blood splashing down on to his shirt front. He pulled a knife from his belt. "So you like blood? Well let's see how you like it when it's yours."

Mandy's heart leapt into her throat as he came forward. The knife blade gleamed and sparkled as the light caught it.

Billy was all set to plunge the knife into her heart when the dry, ratchet clicking of a gun hammer being thumbed back, stopped him.

"Stay your hand, Billy, or I'll drop you where you stand." The words rang out crisp and hard and Billy turned to find that his brother had pulled a gun on him. Billy stared into Roy's eyes and saw that he meant it.

He rubbed blood from his mouth. "What the hell?"

"She belongs to us all. Just 'cause

you couldn't handle her don' mean we can't."

"Roy's right, Billy. You've had your chance; we want ours."

Billy stared from one to the other as the heat of his anger abated under the cold, deadly eye of the Colt.

"Get yourself cleaned up, boy," Roy said. "We'll soften her up for you."

Billy resheathed the knife.

"Damn hell-cat! You're welcome to her," he said sourly, and stamped out of the shack and came face to face with Wes Hardiman. The latter had arrived earlier, circled the shack and, after tethering his horse in the trees, had crept forward.

Wes had found no difficulty in following the tracks of the five horses to the line shack, though the journey had not been without an element of mystery. Twice, in the distance, he had caught a brief glimpse of three riders who appeared to be riding a parallel trail to his. They had been too far away to make any identification, but it made him wonder if he was riding himself into a trap. If they were Tolver's men he was handing himself over on a plate, but he had to try and find out about Mandy, and the occupants of the shack were his only lead.

He put the three riders out of his mind as he crept up on the shack, hearing laughter from within. He was moving cautiously towards the open door when Billy Hapgood made his untimely appearance with his bloodstained chin and shirt.

Billy recovered from the surprise confrontation first; he began yelling and clawing for his gun. Too far away to make a grab for the man, the gun in Wes's hand erupted. The bullet caught Billy in the heart, splintering ribs as it made its destructive way through that organ before exiting just below Billy's left shoulder-blade in a spray of blood and mangled flesh. It stopped Billy's shouts abruptly, spinning him around and slamming him to the sun-baked ground.

In a few brief seconds of surprised silence, Wes had recognized Billy Hapgood from the night he and Ben had rousted the night callers at Mandy's farmhouse. He recognized the thick form of Tate Grissom as the man emerged from the shack squinting in the sunlight, gun half drawn. He staggered a little from the effects of the whiskey, the same whiskey that had drawn him carelessly into the open without thinking. It was his last careless thought. Face grim, Wes fired off two rounds in quick succession. Now that he no longer had the benefit of surprise on his side, he was relying on speed.

Tate took both bullets in his chest. A thick jet of red flew from his lips as the bullets ripped into his lungs and threw him back against the wooden wall next to the door. He slid down the wall into a sitting position, leaving behind a trail of red, and toppled sideways; dead before his head hit the ground.

Roy Hapgood, self-preservation highest

on his list of priorities, leapt up from the table and darted to a position behind Mandy as Wes sprang into the shack and threw himself to one side. Roy Hapgood fired two ineffectual shots in Wes's wake, but the table protected Wes. Only Clem Carson had a good view of Wes, but Clem's hands were in the air and, by now, Wes was up at a half crouch one eye on the thin cowhand.

"I ain't drawing, mister," he screeched fearfully, earning a lip-curled sneer from Roy.

"Allus was a yella dog, Clem, 'less you was back-shootin'," Roy snarled, but his attention was on Wes. "Heard you was dead, freightman."

"Shouldn't believe all you hear," Wes called back. He had found Mandy, but he couldn't fire without hitting her.

"You got two seconds to toss your gun out or the girl gets it." Roy held the end of the gun barrel against the side of Mandy's head, an ugly smile filling his face. He was holding all the aces in this game.

"Then in three seconds you'll be dead," Wes called back bleakly, causing the smile to slip from Roy's face. He had not been expecting that answer and was temporarily thrown.

"Shoot the bastard, Clem, you kin see him," Roy bellowed, but Roy kept his hands well above his head.

"I ain't drawing to no full hand," he shouted back.

"I knew it was a mistake bringing you," Roy grated angrily, swung the gun on to Clem and pulled the trigger. Clem gave a scream as blood spread rapidly across his shirt front just above his belt buckle. Clutching his stomach and moaning Clem fell back into the corner and slid to the floor.

It was over in seconds and once more the barrel was at Mandy's head.

"I've a feeling you wouldn't want her blood on your conscience, freightman," Roy called out.

"Don't do it, Wes," Mandy cried out.

With a sinking feeling Wes knew the man was right. It was stupid really, for the man would have to kill them both anyway. Slowly Wes rose to his feet and tossed his Colt on to the table top before raising his hands to shoulder level and giving Mandy an apologetic smile.

Smiling broadly Roy straightened from behind Mandy and moved to one side turning the gun on Wes.

"This time we'll make real sure you're dead," he gloated, and Wes tensed his body as Roy's finger began to tighten on the trigger.

The shot that rang out made Wes start though not from the impact of a bullet. It was Roy who was slammed back against the bunk bed, arms flung out sideways along the edge of the upper bunk to support his sagging body, blood darkening the front of his shirt. He gave his killer an incredulous stare before crumpling to the floor.

Clem Carson let the gun fall from a nerveless hand.

"Ain't right to shoot a friend," he moaned accusingly at the still form of Roy, then fell sideways and lay still.

Wes leapt across to Mandy and quickly pulled the ropes that held her free. She staggered, white-faced to her feet and threw herself into Wes's arms, kissing and hugging him.

"I thought you were dead," she sobbed.

"So did I and I ain't too sure about Ben." He gently broke her hold and pushed hair from her face feeling the wetness of tears on his fingers. "I've got to find him."

She nodded dumbly. He grabbed up his gun from the table and steered her towards the door.

Stumbling out into the bright sunlight, glad to be away from the stench of blood that filled the shack, Mandy gave a small scream and clutched at Wes, both coming to an abrupt halt.

Before them three, grim-faced strangers clad in dark, dusty range clothes, sat astride their mounts; in their hands they held shot-guns that were levelled unwaveringly at the two.

10

WORK had been called to a halt at the rock face when it was seen that the final tons of rock blasted from the mountain did not contain the elusive treasure. Up on the stone ramparts of the wall the guards had been doubled. The prisoners, with nothing better to do, sat around in silent groups, waiting. They all knew, without actually voicing it, that they had reached the end of their labours.

"What are they waiting for?" Glen Meachen asked tautly, as he sat with Pete and Ben. The tension that he felt was mirrored in the other workers, setting faces and filling eyes with dread. The inevitable moment that they had been slowly working towards was here. Ben now knew how a prisoner sentenced to death must feel on the morning he is to die. He didn't like the feeling.

"The boss man I expect," Pete growled. "Tolver."

A man came across, leg irons clanking, tattered shirt flapping about his thin chest.

"They ain't gonna kill us are they?" he whined. "I mean, they gotta let us go now." There was a thin sheen of sweat on his face. Jeremiah Stubbs had been one of the first to be taken. A drummer selling patent medicines, he had come to Dry Ridge to sell his wares to the gullible only to end up here. Then he had been forty pounds overweight. His eyes searched the faces of the three.

"Sure, Stubbs, they're bound to let us go," Pete said heavily, without conviction, and the man went away muttering to himself.

Ben stared down at the irons on his legs with angry frustration. Blood caked the flimsy strips of shirt he had tied about his feet for protection, oozing from the raw flesh above his ankles where the manacles had rubbed.

It was later on in the morning that the clink of hammers reached their ears and, looking up, they saw tiny figures, high up on the blasted mountain face, attached by ropes, making holes for more dynamite charges.

"Now what do you suppose they're doing that for?" Glen asked, puzzled. Ben had a sudden, nasty idea but said nothing. In any event it cheered up Stubbs for it meant that the fateful moment had been averted. Clearing rock was better than chewing lead.

The morning had grown old by the time Thad Tolver put in an appearance. With Ace Reynolds at his side the pair were flanked by Red, the massive Ox and half a dozen rifle-toting guards. The party approached the prisoners.

"Well boys, it seems that our little partnership has come to an end," Tolver announced. "Can't keep you boys on if'n the work's not there." He grinned darkly and there were smiles from those about him.

"Do it!" he snapped at Red, and turned away.

"There you have it gentlemen. If you'd be so kind as to move back to the cave." He gave a charming smile. The prisoners looked nervously from one to the other.

"What's going on?" Stubbs called out.

"The end of the road, me bucko."

"You're going to kill us!" Stubbs screamed.

"No, we'll let the mountain do that," Red replied, his eyes flickering up to where earlier men had been planting dynamite charges, and the terrible realization of what those charges were for hit the other prisoners.

"You can't bury us alive!" Stubbs screamed. Red gave a nod to Ox and the big man and the guards moved menacingly towards the huddled prisoners. "I ain't dying for you," Stubbs yelled at Pete. "We found the treasure, it's here!" he shouted.

"Stubbs!" Pete shouted. "Keep your

mouth shut." But it was too late, Thad Tolver had heard the shout and was already on his way back.

"What do you mean you've found it?"

"They found it." Stubbs indicated Pete and Glen.

"They hid it. Please, let me go, I won't say anything." His voice became a whining plea.

Tolver grabbed Stubbs' tattered shirt front.

"I knew it was here. Where is it?"

"They buried it in the wall over there. Please, Mr Tolver."

Tolver threw the man roughly aside and moved across to Pete and Glen.

"I might've known you two'd try something like this. So you found it, eh? Well now you find it again, an' just to make sure you do." He pulled his gun, turned on Stubbs and put a bullet through the man's head, blowing half the skull away in a gory explosion of bone and brain. There was a fever in Tolver's eyes as he turned again on Pete. "Do you need any more persuading?"

Pete stared at Tolver coolly.

"You're gonna kill us anyway," he grated back. "You want it, you find it."

Tolver glared at the man.

"You'll die all right," he hissed. "How long have you had the treasure?"

"Since Ray Mallinson escaped," Pete replied, getting some small pleasure from the dumbstruck look on the other's face.

"I might have known," Tolver groaned. He glared hatefully at Pete. "What did you hope to gain? A little more time and the hope that someone would come along and rescue you?" Tolver's face cracked in a smile. "I guess it almost worked," he said with grudging admiration and his eyes fell on Ben. "Maybe would've done, happen him an' his friend were a little smarter." The smile dropped from his face. In a swift movement that took them all by surprise, Tolver whipped the barrel of his gun across Pete Mullin's right cheek, opening the flesh in a deep, red gash. With a cry of pain Pete went down.

Ben started forward but a guard barred his way thrusting the end of a rifle barrel under his throat.

Tolver straddled the moaning man.

"Very clever, but not clever enough. What you gotta remember is that dying can be easy or hard. Maybe you won't talk, but what about the rest of your friends? Pain has a way of loosening the tongue an' I hear tell Ox is an expert in pain. Reckon if'n you listen to a few of your friends screaming for a while you'll be willing to tell me all I wanna know."

"Bastard!" Pete mouthed, around a hand to his face.

"Ain't I just?" Tolver agreed. "Get me that treasure, now!"

Glen helped Pete to his feet and Pete turned pain-racked eyes on Ben.

"Best give him what he wants," Ben said sullenly. Whichever way you looked at it, Thad Tolver had the winning hand.

"I know where it is," Glen spoke up. "I'll need some help to dig it out."

Tolver glanced at Ben and Pete.

"Your two partners will help. Get the rest to the cave."

"Pete can't dig now you've busted his face up, Glen protested.

"Then he'll die now," Tolver said.

"I'll manage," Pete said, right eye pushed shut by the fierce swelling of his broken cheekbone.

While the guards herded the rest of the prisoners to the cave Ben, Pete and Glen were escorted to the rock wall.

"Don't stall for time," Tolver warned. "If'n I think you're playing me for the fool again, I'll start having your friends shot."

* * *

With a sinking heart Wes stared at the three. In the shading brims of their dark hats their faces were bleak and hard and he was in no doubt that these were the same three he had spotted twice, in the distance, on the trail in.

Wes still clutched his gun, but it was at the end of a hanging arm, pointing at the ground. He was in no doubt of what the outcome would be if he tried to raise the gun into a firing position, so he remained still and waited for the three to make the next move.

The centre rider nodded to the man on his left. The rider slid from his mount, circled the two and entered the shack. He emerged twenty seconds later and took up a position behind the two.

"All dead, Will."

The one called Will gave a chilly smile. He wore a drab, brown poncho over his upper body.

"You appear to have had one hell of a time, boy."

"Can't take all the credit. Two of your friends shot each other," Wes replied coldly.

"Friends?" Will seemed genuinely puzzled.

"You work for Tolver don't you?"

"Would appear so," Will agreed. "Leastways, seems a fella with that handle has been spreading our name about."

Wes frowned.

"I ain't sure I know what you mean."

"The name's Slater, Will Slater, an' these are my brothers, Jeb an' Frank. Seems that me an' my brothers have been raiding an' killing in this area. Heard 'bout it while we wus in Oregon so figured we'd better ride down an' see jus' what we've been up to. Ran into Lyle Rance in Dry Ridge toting a sheriff's star an' knew something bad was going down. He gave us the name afore he died."

"You killed him?" Wes blurted out.

"He tried to throw down on Frank." He nodded to the rider on his right. "What can you tell us 'bout this jasper Tolver, boy?"

Thad Tolver had been covering up

his own dirty work by laying the blame on a bunch of genuine outlaws. What he had not reckoned on was those same outlaws hearing about it and coming down to see what was going on. The grim irony of it appealed to Wes.

"Big rancher in these parts. Runs with a gunsel by the name of Ace Reynolds. Those were some of Tolver's boys." Wes caught a flicker of interest in Will Slater's eyes at the mention of Reynolds' name and a look passed between Will and Frank.

"Life sorta gets interesting," Will murmured. "And just who might you be, boy?"

"Wes Hardiman and this is Miss Fuller. They burnt her out last night and took her captive. Reckon it would have been told as another raid by the Slater boys."

"Sort of figured it that way when we saw the flames last night. Heard riders take off but it was too dark to follow, then you showed up an' we waited to see what you would do."

"So it was you following me?"

"Looked to be heading in the direction the riders took, so we followed."

"So what happens now?" Wes asked tautly.

"Reckon we pay this Tolver a visit," Will said.

"And what about us?" Wes tightened his grip on his Colt as he spoke.

Will Slater pointed the shot-gun at the sky, resting its wooden stock on his right thigh.

"Ain't got no argument with you an' the lady, but we'uns ain't no murdering raiders. Bank here an' there an' a train or two." He shrugged. "Figure one day we'll git shot or hung, but we'd sure take it personal if'n we was hung for something we didn't do. Pity you killed them fellas; they could've answered a few questions for us."

Wes slid his Colt back into its holster.

"Maybe we could help each other," he suggested.

"Speak your piece, boy, we're listening."

* * *

The chest that held Cordoba's Treasure looked disappointingly small to Tolver's eyes. Made of dark wood and bound with strips of studded metal it was no more than 24″ × 18″ × 18″. Tolver was expecting something on a much larger scale and turned suspicious eyes on Pete Mullins and Glen Meachen.

"Is this all of it?" he demanded harshly.

"One chest is all that we ever saw," Glen said wearily. "Ask the other men."

"What's the matter, Tolver, reality not matching up to your dreams?" Ben jeered.

Tolver glared at Ben, but did not rise to the bait. He hunkered down before the chest and tugged at a big ornate padlock that locked it.

"How did Mallinson get the pendant

from the chest?" he demanded of Pete.

"Ray had a way with locks," Pete said painfully. "They had a way of opening whenever he was around."

Ben knew that to be true. Ray Mallinson had been a master lock-picker; part of the reason the colonel had employed him.

Tolver rose to his feet brushing dust from his hands.

"Take them to join their friends," he said to Red and, glancing across at Ben's set face, added, "an' if'n any of 'em resist; shoot 'em." He turned to the two guards standing next to the black-garbed, Ace Reynolds. "Get this to the wagon."

As guards moved on the three and began ushering them with prodding rifle butts towards the cave, Ben called, "Ain't you gonna open it, Tolver? Let Red here see what he an' his men have been risking their necks for?"

A rifle butt drove Ben to his knees and Red appeared before his pain-dazed eyes.

"You talk too much, me bucko," Red cried.

"Listen to me," Ben began, and the next second he was struck heavily across the shoulders and sent forward on to his hands. A booted foot slammed into his ribs and sent him rolling over on to his back, a groan breaking from his lips. Against the dazzle of blue sky he saw the huge figure of Ox looming over him, hickory cudgel raised.

With an effort Ben rolled completely over, the sharp stones of the ground biting cruelly into his back. He heard the cudgel crack savagely against the earth and Ox's roar of rage. Ignoring the pain Ben came awkwardly to his feet and faced the lumbering Ox. Hampered by the leg irons Ben stood his ground and faced Ox in a half crouch, fingers curled and splayed ready to grab. The savage light of battle blazed in Ben's grey eyes, reflected a cold half-smile that flicked up the corners of his ragged-bearded lips. "Come on then, fat man," he coaxed.

Guards moved forward to surround Ben while Red stepped in front of Ox.

"Gentlemen, gentlemen," Red said soothingly. "Let's not be wasting time."

"He's mine," Ox grated, glaring at Red.

"Looks like you'll never know if'n you can take me, fat boy," Ben goaded. "Seems you got all these fellas wi' guns to protect you."

Ox's face grew scarlet with suppressed rage. He pushed forward against Red's restraining hand.

"Forget him, Ox, he's taunting you," the Irishman said placatingly. "Let the mountain take care of him."

"Sure, fat boy, let the mountain do what you couldn't," Ben jeered. "And you, Irishman, how much is Tolver paying you? Once that mountain comes down on our heads you'll all be murderers an' the law ain't gonna stop looking for us. You'll spend the rest of your days looking over your shoulders.

I sure hope Tolver's paying you well. I hear tell that Cordoba's Treasure is worth millions. I sure hope you're getting your fair share of it. Or maybe you've got a special deal with Tolver, Red? Happen you'll be OK, but the rest of your boys . . . ?" Ben spread his hands and laughed.

He eyed the guards facing him reading indecision in their eyes. "Once you become murderers there ain't no turning back. I just hope they're paying you enough."

"Very clever, Mr Travis," Red called mockingly, and clapped his hands. "If it's a foight you be wanting, then a foight you'll get, but it'll be your last. Take the irons off him."

* * *

Wes felt that needless time was lost in going to the Tolver ranch, but after hearing his story, Will Slater insisted. He was anxious to face Tolver, but all they found was a frightened Chinese cook. To make matters worse, Mandy insisted on riding with them, refusing to be left behind. She had a stake in finding Tolver too. In the end Wes could not refuse her and so the five headed for the mountains.

Wes pushed hard to make up for lost time and by midday they had reached the point where the high and low trails met. He shivered at the thought of what the low trail had led him into and prayed that the high trail was more friendly.

11

A VICIOUS grin split Ox's broad, stubble-lined face as he faced Ben, slapping the end of his hickory cudgel into the palm of his left hand. With all the prisoners now in the cave the two had the rock-littered area to themselves. Free of the restricting leg irons Ben moved painfully on his rag-bound feet.

The two circled slowly, each waiting for the other to make the first move and it was not until they had made a complete circle that Ox lunged in, lashing with the cudgel. He came in faster than Ben thought possible, the hickory cudgel cutting the air with a dull whistle scant inches from Ben's nose.

Ben leapt backwards, wincing, his sore feet protesting painfully at the sudden move. Ox's smile broadened at the sight of pain lines creasing Ben's face.

"I'm gonna enjoy this," he rasped throatily at Ben.

"You'll need more than a hickory twig to do that," Ben replied. His mouth was dry, heart beating rapidly in his broad chest.

"Gonna bust yer spine," Ox cooed. "Gonna lay you on your back so you kin see the rocks come down on your face. You ain't gonna die easy, boy."

"You planning to jaw me to death, fat boy?" Ben taunted.

The smirk left Ox's face. He was not used to people facing him down. His size generally filled them with fear and that was what he preyed on, but this opponent did not exhibit such fear and that made him feel uneasy. He charged at Ben again swinging the cudgel, but this time Ben was ready.

He caught the cudgel on his left forearm and, even though it was only beginning the downward swing, it jarred his arm from elbow to shoulder. A surge of adrenalin washed through Ben. All the pent-up anger that had been boiling within him for days came to the surface. He drove his right fist deep into Ox's mid-section.

The breath whooshed from Ox's parted lips in a foul-smelling breeze as the blow jolted his body. Ben fisted his left hand and swung it down and across. It rammed into the side of Ox's jaw snapping his head to one side, then a second cross from his right hand snapped the head the other way jerking Ox about like a rag doll.

Ox staggered back, the cudgel falling from his hand, a glazed look in his eyes. He shook his head and managed, more by luck then judgement, to block Ben's next punch and throw one of his own. It scraped under Ben's chin and ran up the side of his face with enough power to stagger Ben back; painful but not damaging.

Ox charged forward, head lowered and rammed his balding pate hard into Ben's midriff. Caught off balance it was like being hit by a battering ram. Ben was thrown backwards, the air driven from his body. He hit the ground hard with his shoulder-blades and back of head and saw flashes of red fire through the welter of pain that flared through his head. Ox let out a roar of triumph, hefted a section of rock that must have weighed at least forty pounds, and advanced on the sprawled, winded Ben.

Through dazed, pain-watering, eyes Ben saw the bulky shape of Ox loom over his arms raised, and rolled to one side.

The rock slab broke in half as it hit the ground where scant seconds before Ben's head had been. On his feet Ben rubbed his eyes to clear them and found that Ox was almost on him.

The man came in low, wrapped thick arms about Ben and, thrusting the top of his head under Ben's chin, forcing the other's head back, began to squeeze. This was one of Ox's favourite moves. If he twisted his head sideways and placed his ear against his victim's upper chest he could hear, above the thundering beat of a terrified heart, bones cracking. It was a sound he liked to hear.

Ox managed to trap Ben's arms at his sides but above the elbow joints. As he began to squeeze, Ben filled his lungs, clenched his fists and brought his lower arm up, expanding his biceps and applying counter pressure.

The two stood there locked together, neither appearing to move as each applied pressure. Sweat exploded over Ben's face. He turned his face to the sky lifting it away from the upward thrust of the other's head. Slowly, teeth gritted, Ben began to push outward with his arms forcing Ox's clenched-together hands apart.

Ox grunted and panted, sweat rolling down his face. The guards and prisoners looked on in silent awe as the two strained to gain the upper hand in a display of raw, animal strength. Ox had never been beaten before. He had fought others of a comparable size to Ben and beaten them, but this time he had met his match. He could feel his hands being pulled apart and there was nothing he could do about it.

Ben felt the hands parting at his back and applied even more pressure, the blood pounding in his ears. Finally the crushing hold broke and Ox staggered back, a bewildered look in his eyes. The effort had taken a toll of both men. Ben exhaled with a mighty hiss and dropped to one knee gulping fresh, clean air into his burning lungs. His arms ached. He rose almost wearily to his feet, rubbing sweat from his eyes. The back-breaking toil and deprivation of the past twenty-four hours had taken the edge off his enormous strength and he knew that if he was to come out of this alive he would have to do something very soon.

He moved forward purposefully and then came to a halt, blood chilling in his veins. Ox had pulled some objects from his pockets. Similar to the nail blocks he had used in the arm wrestling, these had rawhide straps attached enabling Ox to fit them over his hands in a vicious variation of the knuckleduster. Hands clenched, Ox grinned wickedly as he faced Ben.

* * *

Red had followed Thad Tolver before the fight had begun, heading for the hut that Tolver had disappeared into, passing a flat-bed wagon with a canvas top where a group of Tolver's cowboys were busily lashing the chest securely into position for the journey back to the ranch.

Ben's words had struck a chord of distrust in his mind, fanned the flames of greed and suddenly Red had a great desire to see what the chest contained. If it contained the fabulous wealth that legend spoke of, then he and his men deserved a share above the money Tolver had promised them.

Red signalled to a group of miners

to follow him, preferring to face Tolver with a little weight at his back. A few curious eyes followed their progress into the hut, but soon lost interest.

Tolver looked up from behind a battered table as he slopped whiskey into a couple of glasses as Red and ten of the miners squeezed in and the door was shut.

"Are you not going to open the chest, Mr Tolver?" Red asked blandly, as he stopped before the table.

"Later," Tolver said abruptly. "Don't worry, Red, you and your boys'll get what's owing." He passed a glass to the hut's only other occupant; Ace Reynolds, the gunman.

"To be sure, Mr Tolver, you're a generous man, but I'm thinking that perhaps the boys deserve a little bonus?" A general murmur of agreement followed his words.

Tolver stiffened and eyed Red angrily. "We made a deal, Mahonney."

"No mention was made of killing. It'll be murder when the mountain comes down on the poor souls you abducted to do your mining for you. We were only hired to oversee them." Red smiled. "So you see, Mr Tolver, a little extra would guard against a slip of the tongue in the wrong ear."

A series of expressions passed across Tolver's face. He fingered a cigar to his lips and lit it.

"Maybe we can come to some arrangement," he agreed finally.

"'Tis a wise man you are, Mr Tolver. Half the contents of the chest."

"Half?" Tolver shouted wildly, and stared at Red.

"Very generous of you to offer," Red replied smoothly. He had an eye on the gunman, but Reynolds remained impassive and expressionless, leaning nonchalantly against the rear wall, cradling a glass in both hands, looking on but taking no part. He would do nothing unless ordered by Tolver.

"It would appear that you have all the high cards, Mahonney," Tolver said heavily. "Your men are armed and I take it you have a gun?"

"A little insurance," Red replied, withdrawing a hand clutching a tiny, double-barrelled derringer from his coat pocket.

"A cautious man," Tolver commented with a half smile.

"Cautious men live longer," Red replied. "Shall we go out to the wagon and complete our little deal?"

"Sure, why not?" Tolver said with a shrug.

"You and Reynolds first," Red prompted, and this time Tolver smiled broadly.

"You sure are a cautious man, Mahonney."

Doubts flooded into Red's mind. Tolver was taking it all far too calmly and that worried him.

The red-haired Irishman looked around suspiciously as he and the others followed Tolver and the silent gunman out into the bright sunlight.

Something was not quite right, Red could feel it, but not pin it down.

Apart from two cowboys standing idly by the wagon, none of Tolver's other men were in sight.

"Don't try anything, Mr Tolver," Red warned, "'Tis you who'll be first to die."

"I intend to die of old age in bed," Tolver called back.

As they approached the wagon, the rear flaps hiding its contents from prying eyes, Tolver and Reynolds peeled apart and took up position, facing the miners, either side of the wagon. Red brought his men to a halt.

"You were right, Red, cautious men do live longer; it's the stupid ones who get the'selves killed. Reckon you musta figured me for stupid for not thinking you'd try something like this." A sneer spread across Tolver's face and he nodded across to Reynolds and together they opened the rear flaps.

Red's mouth fell open in shocked surprise as he stared down the multiple barrels of a tripod-mounted, Catling gun.

"A little insurance of my own," Tolver sang out. "It's been waiting for this day ever since we came here and you knew nothing about it." Tolver jeered, then shouted harshly to the shadowy form of the gun's operator. "Kill them!"

* * *

Ben ran a hand across his dry lips as he saw the cushions of nail points thrusting out a good inch from Ox's clenched fists. One touch from those and flesh and muscle would be ripped in agonizing chunks from his body. Even a glancing blow would do irreparable damage.

"Come on, big fella, see what ol' Ox has got for you," Ox taunted, moving cautiously forward, his confidence growing as Ben backed nervously away from him. Ox punched the air playfully between them. "What's the matter, big fella?" Ox wheezed.

Ben peered desperately around. The ground was littered with rocks. A piece a foot square and perhaps three inches thick caught his eye. He grabbed it up and held it before him ready to block any blows that Ox might throw. So intent was he, on the approaching Ox, that he failed to see one of the guards move up behind him. He only became aware of him when the butt of a rifle was slammed viciously into the small of his back.

Agony ripped through Ben's back and drove needles of white-hot pain deep into his brain, tearing a harsh cry from his lips as he sank to his knees.

"Now that ain't fair," the guard declared, grinning.

The rock slab dropped from Ben's nerveless hands as he knelt, back arched, hands still raised as though he was holding the rock slab. Caught in a welter of paralyzing pain he could not move. Only his eyes worked and they watched helplessly as Ox loomed over him and drew back a meaty fist.

"Any last words, big boy?" he hissed, spittle flecking his lips.

Ben's lips ripped away from his teeth, he raised his face to the sky and let out a wild, rebel yell as he brought all his concentration to bear on tearing down the walls of pain that held him prisoner. Adrenalin pumped, his fists balled and he rose to his feet to face Ox. The yell had stopped the big man, fist poised, wiping the grin from his face. Its primitive cadences echoed about the craggy rock faces focusing all eyes on the two protagonists.

Ben's eyes were on Ox, chips of hard, grey flint that had lost the light of humanity and, for the first time ever, Ox felt the cold, mind-freezing chill of fear. He threw the belated punch and this time Ben did not flinch or draw back. He parried the blow with an arm and then, raising both hands, fingers straight, he chopped down on both sides of Ox's thick neck in a fierce double blow.

To Ox it felt as though he had caught his neck in a closing door. Pain flared through his thick shoulders and up to both ears. Ben grabbed the man's wrists before he had time to recover.

"I don't think you're gonna enjoy this," he grated, and brought both of Ox's wrists together and drove them up under the man's chin, jamming the nail blocks that Ox wore deep into the man's throat.

Ox screamed hoarsely, tore himself free from Ben's grip, staggered and fell backwards. The fall made him throw out his arms automatically, and the nail blocks on his hands came away with thick pads of raw, ragged-edged flesh attached.

Blood bubbled from his mouth and ran in scarlet streams down his shirt front from the terrible wounds in his throat as he heaved himself to his feet. He managed one tottering step before sinking to his knees, blood filling his lungs and then he fell forward, choking and jerking in his own gore until, with a final convulsive jerk, death took up residence and he lay still.

Ben wheeled away and threw himself at the guard who had rifle butted him earlier. The man, shocked at what had happened to Ox, failed to respond to the threat until it was too late. Ben ripped the rifle from his grasp and drove the butt between his eyes, felling the man instantly.

The other guards, caught by surprise, were a little late in reacting to the sudden turn of events; not so the prisoners. Crowded to the front of the cave, Pete Mullins saw his chance as Ben went for the guard. The cave guards had their backs to the prisoners; Pete signalled Glen Meachen and both dashed out as quick as their manacled legs would allow and threw themselves on the unsuspecting men. The other prisoners followed scooping up rocks and stones to use as weapons.

As the prisoners made a desperate

bid for freedom Ben threw the rifle to his shoulder and levered off a shot that sent a guard spinning to the ground, the top of his head blown away. The guards, made up of Red's miners, were only six in number. Seeing two of their number go down before Ben and two more overcome by prisoners, the remaining two lost heart. They were not fighting men. They took to their heels and ran towards the wall.

Pete Mullins, grinning broadly, hobbled towards Ben waving a captured rifle in his hands, but the smile wavered and fell away as the sudden growling chatter of rapid gunfire filled the air, mingled with the screams of dying men. He threw Ben a puzzled look.

"What the hell was that?"

"Trouble with a capital T," Ben said grimly. He recognized the distinctive sound for what it was, but before he could elaborate, Glen was pointing to the wall at Ben's back and shouting something. Ben turned to see men with rifles appearing along the top of the wall; a dozen or more. As he looked they levelled their rifles and a chill went through him. The two running guards were gunned down as they scrambled up the slope of the wall, then the rifles were turned on the prisoners.

Sick realization flooded into Ben's mind that this had all been planned: the fact that there were no miners making up the riflemen. The earlier shooting and screams told him that Tolver meant none to survive but his own men.

"Take cover!" he roared and dived to the ground as the riflemen began spraying leaden death in their direction.

12

SOME of the prisoners were too slow in taking cover and Ben saw them go down in a welter of blood as the heavy bullets slammed into their bodies.

Anger ripped through him at the senseless slaughter, brought about by one man's greed. He rolled on to his back behind rocks that barely shielded his big form, clutching the rifle to his chest and waiting as bullets chipped the rocks around him and screamed away into the air.

Pete Mullins crawled across to him, blood trickling from a cut on his left cheek, adding to the damage on his face.

"We lost four," he shouted across to Ben. "They never stood a chance."

Four, plus Stubbs earlier, meant that they had been reduced by half.

"An' we ain't much better off," Ben called back. He rolled on to his front and levered off a quick, unaimed shot; a token gesture. A dozen were returned throwing rock splinters into his face. Unless a miracle occurred they were all doomed.

Gab Little stood on the rock wall, his thin, dark face wreathed in a happy smile. He worked a cigar-stub from one side of his wide mouth to the other as he levered shots at the pinned-down men. He felt a sudden pain in his back that made him jerk, but he didn't have time to consider its implication until the front of his chest exploded outwards in a gory, jetting spray of blood, bone and lung. He was thrown forward to slide and tumble like a broken doll down the sloping face of the wall, dead long before he reached the bottom.

Ben glimpsed the falling man and saw others on the wall turning and firing at someone whom Ben could not see. Not knowing what was happening,

Ben saw his chance and took it. Rising to his knees he opened up with his rifle and scored a direct hit on another rifleman. From beyond the wall the faint rumble of hoofs mingled with the crack and crash of the rifles.

Panic and confusion hit the riflemen as suddenly they found themselves being shot at from both sides. They were breaking up, leaping down the inner face of the wall to escape whatever was happening on the other side. The hammer of Ben's rifle clicked on an empty chamber and he threw it down in disgust.

Pete and Glen cut loose with their rifles at the fleeing figures. Two went down but two others scrambled over the wall at the far side. The shooting had become sporadic and none aimed at the prisoners. The sound of hoofs had stopped and silence fell.

The three moved together and a fourth emerged from the rocks to join them, all that remained alive of the ten prisoners.

"What's going on?" Glen asked nervously.

A figure appeared on the top of the rock wall. Glen threw up his rifle, but Ben knocked it aside.

"Hold your fire," he cried, and stared with disbelief at the figure. "I don't believe it," he breathed, as a slow smile spread across his face. Pete was smiling painfully too and Glen looked at them in bewilderment.

On the rock wall Wes Hardiman waved his rifle and began scrambling down to join them. Three more figures appeared and Ben's eyes popped as he recognized a fourth: Mandy Fuller.

"Goddam cavalry's arrived," Ben breathed, limping forward to meet Wes. "Man that's been under a few hundred tons of rock ain't got the right to look as good as you," Ben bawled out, gripping his partner's hand in welcome. "Figured you for dead."

"You look as though you are," Wes replied. "Good to see you alive, big fella." His eyes travelled to Pete Mullins as the man hobbled over, grimacing at the man's battered face.

"How you doing, Pete?" he asked doubtfully.

"All the better for seeing you, Wes. This here's Glen Meachen and Chuck Simpkins. Rest are all dead."

Wes nodded grimly and Ben threw a look at the three men on the wall.

"Who are your friends, Wes?"

"Just some boys with a grudge to settle against Thad Tolver. He sorta took their names in vain." He gave a wintry smile. "The Slater boys. I'll tell you 'bout it later. Let's get these fellas unchained, then we got some riding to do to catch Tolver."

"He's got the treasure," Ben said.

"Not for long," Wes replied, as he levered a shell into the breech of his Winchester and placed the end of the barrel against the links of the chain between Pete's ankles and pulled the trigger. Two shots later both Pete and Chuck had the freedom to walk normally. "Can't do nothing 'bout the ankle irons 'till we reach town," he apologized.

"Long as I can fork a horse I'm happy," Pete declared.

Mandy greeted Ben with a hug as he reached the top of the wall.

"We thought you were dead," she cried in relief.

"They tried," Ben replied.

"Where's Tolver?" Will Slater spoke up.

"He was here just afore you arrived," Ben said.

"We heard the Gatling," Wes voiced, "but don't see it none, though there was a sight of dead bodies near that shack."

"That was Tolver paying Red and his men a little surprise bonus," Ben said bleakly. "He had a wagon. He told his men to get the chest with the treasure in to the wagon."

"Reckon that boy's getting away while we stand here jawing," Will Slater growled.

"We got the time," Pete spoke up.

"He's taken the lower trail. Circles 'round the mountain an' comes out near to the one you boys came in on. We can take the top trail and git there ahead of him."

"Sounds good to me," Wes said. "There are some horses saddled in the corral. Reckon they were for these boys when they'd done with you. Guess they won't be needing 'em now."

"Which 'minds me," Ben broke in. "They were setting charges in the cliff earlier to bury our bodies. Reckon Tolver will be waiting to hear the explosion."

"Best not disappoint him then," Wes said casually.

They headed for the corral that lay just beyond the cabins, Mandy, white-faced, averting her eyes as they passed the still, sprawled bodies of Red and his miners. The Slaters waited in frustrated silence as Wes and Ben took time to do a quick search of the buildings in case anyone was hiding in them. All they found was Ben's boots and hat tossed in a corner of the storehouse, but no sign of his gunbelt.

In the bunkhouse Pete and Chuck found fresh clothes to wear and a supply of water to slake a thirst that seemed never ending. Leaving the three, Wes went in search of the fuses to the dynamite charges. He found them trailing up a thirty-foot narrow cut that fissured the rock wall before they looped across the rock face to the planted charges; Tolver sure had everything all worked out neatly.

"If'n we don't make a move soon that boy's gonna be long gone," Frank complained, as Wes returned.

"Then let's move out," Wes said crisply, "and take any extra horses. I'll get the fuses lit an' follow directly."

In a long string led by the Slaters they moved out, Ben leading the remaining, saddled animals. Wes entered the storehouse and rolled out a barrel of kerosene. He stove in the top with the butt of his rifle and turned the barrel on its side letting its pungent-smelling contents flood about the bodies that already the flies were building up on, rising in dark, buzzing clouds as he approached. It would be a pleasure to see Tolver on the gallows after this display of callous indifference.

Wes rode his paint to the cut, touched off the fuses and then rode back through the camp tossing a lighted match on to the pool of kerosene. It ignited with a dull crump and engulfed the bodies in a sea of fire.

The others were waiting on the trail above the timberline.

"Figured you'd liked it so much down there you'd decided to stay," Will Slater commented, and frowned at the column of smoke that was rising above the trees.

"Reckon they deserved better than being left to the flies and buzzards," was all Wes said.

"How long afore she blows?" Ben asked, and at that moment an explosion, softened by distance, rumbled on the air. It was followed by a second and then a third. The ground beneath them shook and, from the distant rock face, mushrooms of white smoke and dust erupted upwards carrying with it huge slabs of rock that whirled high into the air before falling to earth. The whole top of what had once been a mountain shivered and with a roar began to crumble. Seconds later the sound buffeted their ears like a roll of endless thunder that had their mounts moving restlessly beneath them. What had once been a high mountain valley was now a tomb that buried the dead of Thad Tolver's greed.

As the echoes of the explosions faded Wes knee'd his mount forward.

"Let's go and welcome ol' Thad," he said bleakly.

* * *

Small stone fragments shaken loose by the multiple explosions rained down on the wagon, rattling like hail on the canvas top. Tolver shortened the reins on the team of four and checked them as the ground shook. He insisted on driving the wagon, the cargo was too valuable to be trusted to less experienced hands. In the rear of the wagon Carl Betts and Hank Brady manned the Gatling gun. Paul Wilks and Stud Hogan rode behind the wagon while Ace Reynolds led the way. All men whom he could trust and he felt safe.

As the rumbling echoes faded away a smile filled Tolver's face. Everything had worked out as he had planned. With Cordoba's Treasure he would become the richest man in Nevada and California put together.

"Lead on, Mr Reynolds," he called out, and Ace Reynolds raised a hand in acknowledgement and knee'd his mount forward.

It was a slow journey through the narrow, twisting canyons that led ever downwards to the plains below, but one in which Tolver could dream of the great days ahead. Already he had plans for renaming Dry Ridge, Tolverville. Mayor of Tolverville and then state governorship; maybe one day, President of the United States. In his mind he could see no goal unobtainable until the tree shattered his dreams and destroyed his illusions of the great things ahead.

There was nothing unusual about the tree. Now that they had descended lower, the steep slopes on either side of the trail had become clothed in sweet-smelling pine; it was just that this particular one lay across the trail, blocking it.

Reynolds rode back to the wagon as Tolver brought it to a halt.

"Trail's blocked," he muttered, eyes flickering around.

"I can see that for myself," Tolver said testily, before bawling, "Wilks, Hogan, git that goddam tree moved." The two riders following the wagon moved forward, urging their mounts to the fallen tree as Tolver hauled a shot-gun from beneath his seat. "I don't like this," he muttered. The wagon rocked a little. Tolver tilted his head back. "Be ready in there when I give the word," he said from the corner of his mouth. The wagon rocked again and something clattered noisily within. Tolver was about to turn in his seat when a voice froze him.

"We meet again, Thad. You sure took your time." Wes rose from behind the fallen tree, Colt Peacemaker held in one hand, a smile on his face.

Thad Tolver's eyes bulged in surprise and disbelief.

"You!" he squawked.

"Throw down your guns and climb down, boys, real easy like," Wes drawled to the two riders. To emphasize his words Glen and Pete sprang into view on either side of him, rifles pointing at the two. "Guess you heard the rumour I was dead too. Sure sorry to disappoint you."

"That goes for me also," Mandy said sweetly, as she came into view and moved to Wes's side.

For Thad Tolver it was like being in the grip of a nightmare. Sweat broke out on his face.

"Do something," he snarled at Reynolds, but the gunman sat with both hands on the saddlehorn and did not move.

"Toss the piece, Tolver, and climb down," Wes called, "or I'll shoot you where you sit an' that'll make me feel a whole heap better. Ain't nothing like dropping half a mountain on a man to make him right ornery."

"Half; you can have half of the treasure," Tolver cried.

"Still think you can buy people, Tolver?" Wes said mockingly. "All of Cordoba's Treasure won't save you from the hangman. Now get down."

Tolver threw the shot-gun aside and climbed down to stand stiffly at the side of the wagon.

"Take it all," Tolver shouted. "It's in the wagon; I'll show you. Reynolds, get the other flap." Tolver's eyes were shining in his sweating face as both jerked the flaps open. "Now!" Tolver screamed.

"You know I just ain't got how this dang thing works," Ben said, smiling over the barrels of the Gatling gun. In the rear of the wagon the two gun operators sat trussed and gagged. "But this here kind fella's been looking after my gun." He pointed his Adams at Tolver.

Tolver staggered away from the wagon, face ashen, a wild look in his eyes.

"You're finished, Tolver. We know you had the Fullers murdered and Doc Holby. You almost got Miss Fuller here, but your boys botched it, and what happened to Sheriff Cates?" Wes's eyes settled on the two cowboys who stood with their hands in the air. "Speak up, boys, it might just save your necks from getting stretched."

"It was Reynolds; he shot him," one of the men said.

"It was the Slaters," Tolver burst out. "Everyone knows it was the Slaters who did the killing. Lyle Rance was on their trail." There was desperation in his voice.

"Rance couldn't trail his own shadow without losing it." A new voice spoke up and Will Slater followed by his two brothers emerged from the trees at the side of the trail.

"Who?" Tolver began.

"You should know these fellas, Tolver," Wes cut in. "They're the Slater boys you've been blaming everything on an' they've sure been looking forward to meeting you." Wes was enjoying himself watching Tolver sag and wilt with every passing second.

Will Slater ignored Tolver. His eyes were on Reynolds.

"Figured that one day we'd meet agin, Ace. Me an' the boys here bin looking forward to it."

A cold smile filled the gunman's face.

"Three to one. Sure, why not?" Reynolds stood with thumbs hooked in his gunbelt.

"I made the mistake of saving your neck, Ace, I'll be the one to put it right," Will Slater said softly. "Frank and Jeb have been told to keep out of it." Obligingly the two brothers moved away from Will. The sudden, unexpected turn of events left Wes and the others as silent, wondering onlookers. Wes learned later that it was over a woman who had died.

"Make your play, Will," Reynolds hissed. "You always figured you wus faster'n me." He settled into a tense crouch, right hand hovering over the butt of his holstered gun.

Wes found himself tensing in the brittle, charged silence that had built up. When the moment came it could have been missed in the blink of an eye.

In speed of draw Ace Reynolds had the edge, but Will Slater had the experience. Both guns fired together, Reynolds a shade quicker but, as Will drew and fired, he twisted his body sideways to reduce the target area. The bullet from Reynolds' gun tugged at the front of Will's coat as it passed.

Reynolds jerked and staggered as blood blossomed across the front of his shirt, a look of surprise in his eyes. He fought to bring up his sagging gun for a second shot, but Will fired again and again until his gun was empty and Reynolds lay face down in his own blood in the dust.

"That's for Mary," Will murmured, as the tension drained from his face.

A shot rang out, kicking the shot-gun that Tolver was reaching for and Wes thumbed back the hammer warningly.

"Back up, Tolver. I aim to see you dancing at the end of a rope." He clambered over the fallen tree. "We need you to clear Will and his brothers of the killings you done in their name."

Will Slater nodded at Wes. "We're obliged to you, Wes. Reckon you won't be needing us any more, so we'll ride on." He held out a hand and Wes shook it.

"Just don't try robbing Midwest Freight; I'd hate to be the one to come after you," Wes said.

Will smiled. "I'll remember."

"Look, there's enough treasure for us all," Tolver pleaded.

"You're wrong there, Tolver." Pete Mullins came forward. "What's in that chest can be picked up anywhere."

"What do you mean?" Tolver whimpered.

"Be obliged if'n you'd bring that chest out, Ben," Pete called.

A few minutes later the chest sat on the trail.

"Well it sure is heavy," Ben complained.

Pete turned his rifle on the lock, shooting it away and he was grinning as best he could with his battered face as he lifted the lid to reveal that it was filled with rocks.

Tolver, forgetting everything; fell to his knees before the chest and pulled out the rocks. Finally he sank back on his haunches and stared up at Pete.

"Where is it?"

"We took it out, Glen, Ray and I, and hid it in the cave at the bottom of the cliff. It was easier to hide piece by piece. The chest was something different. We filled it with rocks and buried it in the wall. Cordoba's Treasure is still up there only now it's buried under half the mountain." There was a vicious pleasure in his voice as he saw Tolver crumple into a broken, beaten man. Pete looked at Ben. "Sorry we didn't tell you, Ben, but Glen and I were prepared to die to keep the secret, so the less people that knew the better."

"What if Tolver had decided to open the chest?" Wes asked.

Pete shrugged.

"It was a risk; but on the other hand would you open up a chest of treasure in front of the likes of Red and his men? Best to get it out and away before they had time to think about it."

"You wouldn't have used it to bargain for your lives?" Wes raised an eyebrow.

"Tolver couldn't afford to leave any of us alive. Once he had his hands on it he would have killed us anyway no matter what promises he made to get it, so at least we would have died rich." He grinned awkwardly. "Now nobody gets it."

"Well, Colonel Tom told us it was cursed and a lot of men have died for it along the way. Maybe it's best it stays buried," Wes said. "Let's get that tree moved and get out of here. We've got ol' Thad's party to look forward to; his necktie party."

THE END

Other titles in the Linford Western Library:

TOP HAND
Wade Everett

The Broken T was big. But no ranch is big enough to let a man hide from himself.

GUN WOLVES OF LOBO BASIN
Lee Floren

The Feud was a blood debt. When Smoke Talbot found the outlaws who gunned down his folks he aimed to nail their hide to the barn door.

SHOTGUN SHARKEY
Marshall Grover

The westbound coach carrying the indomitable Larry and Stretch headed for a shooting showdown.

FIGHTING RAMROD
Charles N. Heckelmann

Most men would have cut their losses, but Frazer counted the bullets in his guns and said he'd soak the range in blood before he'd give up another inch of what was his.

LONE GUN
Eric Allen

Smoke Blackbird had been away too long. The Lequires had seized the Blackbird farm, forcing the Indians and settlers off, and no one seemed willing to fight! He had to fight alone.

THE THIRD RIDER
Barry Cord

Mel Rawlins wasn't going to let anything stand in his way. His father was murdered, his two brothers gone. Now Mel rode for vengeance.

ARIZONA DRIFTERS
W. C. Tuttle

When drifting Dutton and Lonnie Steelman decide to become partners they find that they have a common enemy in the formidable Thurston brothers.

TOMBSTONE
Matt Braun

Wells Fargo paid Luke Starbuck to outgun the silver-thieving stagecoach gang at Tombstone. Before long Luke can see the only thing bearing fruit in this eldorado will be the gallows tree.

HIGH BORDER RIDERS
Lee Floren

Buckshot McKee and Tortilla Joe cut the trail of a border tough who was running Mexican beef into Texas. They stopped the smuggler in his tracks.

BRETT RANDALL, GAMBLER
E. B. Mann

Larry Day had the choice of running away from the law or of assuming a dead man's place. No matter what he decided he was bound to end up dead.

THE GUNSHARP
William R. Cox

The Eggerleys weren't very smart. They trained their sights on Will Carney and Arizona's biggest blood bath began.

THE DEPUTY OF SAN RIANO
Lawrence A. Keating and Al. P. Nelson

When a man fell dead from his horse, Ed Grant was spotted riding away from the scene. The deputy sheriff rode out after him and came up against everything from gunfire to dynamite.

FARGO: MASSACRE RIVER
John Benteen

The ambushers up ahead had now blocked the road. Fargo's convoy was a jumble, a perfect target for the insurgents' weapons!

SUNDANCE: DEATH IN THE LAVA
John Benteen

The Modoc's captured the wagon train and its cargo of gold. But now the halfbreed they called Sundance was going after it . . .

HARSH RECKONING
Phil Ketchum

Five years of keeping himself alive in a brutal prison had made Brand tough and careless about who he gunned down . . .

FARGO: PANAMA GOLD
John Benteen

With foreign money behind him, Buckner was going to destroy the Panama Canal before it could be completed. Fargo's job was to stop Buckner.

FARGO: THE SHARPSHOOTERS
John Benteen

The Canfield clan, thirty strong were raising hell in Texas. Fargo was tough enough to hold his own against the whole clan.

PISTOL LAW
Paul Evan Lehman

Lance Jones came back to Mustang for just one thing — revenge! Revenge on the people who had him thrown in jail.

HELL RIDERS
Steve Mensing

Wade Walker's kid brother, Duane, was locked up in the Silver City jail facing a rope at dawn. Wade was a ruthless outlaw, but he was smart, and he had vowed to have his brother out of jail before morning!

DESERT OF THE DAMNED
Nelson Nye

The law was after him for the murder of a marshal — a murder he didn't commit. Breen was after him for revenge — and Breen wouldn't stop at anything . . . blackmail, a frameup . . . or murder.

DAY OF THE COMANCHEROS
Steven C. Lawrence

Their very name struck terror into men's hearts — the Comancheros, a savage army of cutthroats who swept across Texas, leaving behind a bloodstained trail of robbery and murder.

SUNDANCE: SILENT ENEMY
John Benteen

A lone crazed Cheyenne was on a personal war path. They needed to pit one man against one crazed Indian. That man was Sundance.

LASSITER
Jack Slade

Lassiter wasn't the kind of man to listen to reason. Cross him once and he'll hold a grudge for years to come — if he let you live that long.

LAST STAGE TO GOMORRAH
Barry Cord

Jeff Carter, tough ex-riverboat gambler, now had himself a horse ranch that kept him free from gunfights and card games. Until Sturvesant of Wells Fargo showed up.

McALLISTER ON THE COMANCHE CROSSING
Matt Chisholm

The Comanche, McAllister owes them a life — and the trail is soaked with the blood of the men who had tried to outrun them before.

QUICK-TRIGGER COUNTRY
Clem Colt

Turkey Red hooked up with Curly Bill Graham's outlaw crew. But wholesale murder was out of Turk's line, so when range war flared he bucked the whole border gang alone . . .

CAMPAIGNING
Jim Miller

Ambushed on the Santa Fe trail, Sean Callahan is saved by two Indian strangers. But there'll be more lead and arrows flying before the band join Kit Carson against the Comanches.

GUNSLINGER'S RANGE
Jackson Cole

Three escaped convicts are out for revenge. They won't rest until they put a bullet through the head of the dirty snake who locked them behind bars.

RUSTLER'S TRAIL
Lee Floren

Jim Carlin knew he would have to stand up and fight because he had staked his claim right in the middle of Big Ike Outland's best grass.

THE TRUTH ABOUT SNAKE RIDGE
Marshall Grover

The troubleshooters came to San Cristobal to help the needy. For Larry and Stretch the turmoil began with a brawl and then an ambush.

WOLF DOG RANGE
Lee Floren

Will Ardery would stop at nothing, unless something stopped him first — like a bullet from Pete Manly's gun.

DEVIL'S DINERO
Marshall Grover

Plagued by remorse, a rich old reprobate hired the Texas Troubleshooters to deliver a fortune in greenbacks to each of his victims.

GUNS OF FURY
Ernest Haycox

Dane Starr, alias Dan Smith, wanted to close the door on his past and hang up his guns, but people wouldn't let him.

DONOVAN
Elmer Kelton

Donovan was supposed to be dead. Uncle Joe Vickers had fired off both barrels of a shotgun into the vicious outlaw's face as he was escaping from jail. Now Uncle Joe had been shot — in just the same way.

CODE OF THE GUN
Gordon D. Shirreffs

MacLean came riding home, with saddle tramp written all over him, but sewn in his shirt-lining was an Arizona Ranger's star.

GAMBLER'S GUN LUCK
Brett Austen

Gamblers seldom live long. Parker was a hell of a gambler. It was his life — or his death . . .